Hold Onto Me

Before The Light #1
Michael's Story

Hold Onto Me (Before the Light #1)
By
Melyssa Winchester

Copyright © 2014 Melyssa Winchester

To the strongest warrior I know. This one's for you Dad. Thank you for your never ending love and support. I will treasure it just as I do you. Always.

Prologue

Michael

From the very moment of my creation, things for me have always had a beginning, middle and end and there has never been a moment of deviation in between.

I've taken comfort in it being that way. It means I always know what is coming. There can be no surprises or things that do not go according to plan. It allows me to stand beside my father and do what is required of me without doubt or other questionable thoughts bleeding over and ruining things before they have begun.

That is not to say I am against change or do not believe that things that start out in one manner do not have the ability to be changed into something more favorable, because I do. I just do not have the familiarity with it the way my brothers do.

Take Gabriel for instance. If he were put into the position I find myself in, he would be able to adapt easily. He would question it of course, it is his way after all, but he would in time adapt despite it taking him away from his original course of action. It is something I am unable to do.

When Father created us, he did so with specific goals in mind. Even before I knew it myself, he had a purpose for me. I am a warrior. I am the one that due to events in our past, now gets to stand beside him, learning from his vast experience and taking that which I have learned and using it in order to have things be the way he envisions them. I am a fighter above all else and no matter what path I take, I will remain such forever.

My brothers on the other hand, they all have purposes far different than my own. Gabriel is the brother that experiences all things human in nature. He is the one that was given the ability to feel and express and in our time together he has never missed an opportunity to do so. He is the go-to brother for matters pertaining to emotion, so there is no doubt in my mind that of all my brothers, he would be the most understanding of my current plight.

We then have Raphael and Uriel. They are most like me in that they do not go out of their way to experience anything that remotely pertains to the planet we are charged with guarding. They are most comfortable here at home, though I cannot discount Uriel's ability to break through barriers both here and in other plains as it pertains to the darkness my fallen brother has created. Raphael, though he hates admitting to it, has always been the healer. He has no urge to do so in human situations, but both above and below he has the ability to heal with the light he has been given. He is like Gabriel in that regard which should make them closer but because of his personality that is not the case. In that way, he is most like me.

They would not understand what I am experiencing now, though they could prove to be useful in the future when I need to have the memory of this wretched time removed from my memory banks.

I should have been expecting this of course. It's not as if everything I am experiencing now is foreign to me, but when you spent centuries believing what you have been told yet not experiencing it for yourself, you begin to lose hope that you ever will. I did not see this coming and that disturbs me more than the feelings themselves.

Father from the beginning has spoken of the beloved. It is the one being in all of creation that has been made for us. They will be what we are not. They are meant to compliment us in ways that will strengthen us, making us better warriors and lights for the place we call home. For someone like Gabriel, they would be more action oriented than emotionally based and for me, they would be most like my brother is. They would feel things strongly, express themselves emotionally and be my polar opposite yet perfect for me.

I can only liken it to the humans and the way they experience love. There are differences of course, but the feelings that one experiences are quite similar, just more powerful. It is most like the bond between soul-mates in that it can never be broken and once it's been activated, it is as if the two beings truly become one.

In much the same way that my brothers and I garner enjoyment from the way the humans act, it is much the same way with the beloved bond. It has not happened to any of us and because of that it is seen as a fable. A story Father told us that has no place in our reality. It is nothing more than a joke and one that we have exploited for our own enjoyment for centuries.

This is where the line between fable and reality becomes blurred. I can no longer look at it in the manner I have been. It is no longer a joke and I do not believe it will ever be seen as one again. I feel this way because I am experiencing it firsthand. Why it has to happen to me first, when it should be happening to the one brother that feels more than humanly possible is beyond me, but I can no longer ignore that it exists.

I have met my beloved and my way of being, believing in the beginning, middle and end of things has been thrown into a tailspin. Now that I have met her and she has turned my existence on its axis, there can be no going back.

My only hope is, I don't live to regret it.

Chapter One

Faith

I have existed for millennia yet how I came to be never ceases to amaze me.

I often sit back and wonder just what our father had been thinking in creating us and if the level of beauty we get to experience on a day to day basis is in fact real. What we are, how we came to be and where we reside, it is all so magnificent that there are no words in any language that can adequately explain it. What our father has given us is the most beautiful dream brought to life.

It is not without hardships. Nothing worth having ever comes easily, but when you have been blessed with an existence such as the one I continue to live each day, it makes it difficult to focus on them. You want to surround yourself with the true beauty that resides here, instead of focusing on that which you cannot control.

My existence here did not begin in the same way as others like me. I was not brought into the light to be what I am now. I was meant to be something more, or at least that is how Father has explained it to me in the past.

I began this life as pure energy. There were many of us created in much the same way, but only one of us remained that way until such time as she would be used. Those of us that did not fit into the larger picture as Father has seen it became bringers of light.

As much as I love everything as it pertains to the light of my home, there is a sense of accomplishment I get from my position that I would not trade for the world. I am tasked with watching over the humans, reaching out to those that are at their roughest point and smoothing out their edges.

Has every one of my assignments been easy? Have they all worked out the way I expected when I entered into them?

Of course not. I have lost more than a few to the darkness, unable to break through their well constructed walls in order to bring them back into the light, but it has not deterred me from my path. If anything, being unable to save those few serves me well with the ones I am tasked with saving now. It is my hope that the day will come where the risk of losing one will no longer exist and every human will end up where they are meant to.

I can remember the day Father spoke about my purpose would be. At that time, I had been fearful about where I would find myself, another ball of light having been chosen in my place, and had no idea what to expect when I found myself standing before him. As off kilter as I felt, he made every attempt to assuage my fears, letting me know that there was still a purpose for me.

It is the day my existence changed forever.

*****

"Faith, I understand your trepidation, but you have nothing to fear. I called for you because there is much that we need to discuss."

I am sure this is the moment he tells me that because I was not the chosen ball of light, he no longer has any use for me. It is not as if it is a competition, but what other use could there be for a being like myself if not that?

"There are much brighter things in your future, of that I can assure you. As I have said, you my magnificent ball of light, have nothing to worry about."

"What do you require of me, Father?"

"You may not have been the one chosen to alter the landscape of the world, but what you are meant for moving

forward is just as important. It is my hope that in telling you, you agree so that we may move forward and do what is right."

"I believe in the light, what you have created both above and below. I will do whatever I can to make sure that the light continues to live on despite the growing force of the darkness. All you need to do is tell me where you need me."

"Your primary purpose for the time being will be to watch over the humans, in a guardian capacity and the ones that reach their darkest point and feel as though they cannot go forward productively, you will be charged with saving."

It is not unheard of given where we reside for this to be a request. There are angels all throughout Heaven that have been tasked with much the same thing as he is asking of me now. I am just unsure what it is about me that makes me worthy.

"All beings of light are worthy, Faith."

"I do not mean to make it seem that I doubt you. I am just finding it hard to believe that you have this much faith in my ability. Tasking me with something of this magnitude—are you sure?"

"I have never been more sure, Faith. You were created from the purest light imaginable. There is no better place for you than here, doing that which I am asking of you. Your very name alone speaks to it."

*****

I have been doing this for so long that I could not imagine doing something else, losing count just how many souls I have saved and brought back into the light. All I know is that it is what I was meant to do. I may have been born of the purest light ever created, but that was never meant to be my place. This was.

As it is with every job, it is not without its disadvantages.

What I do, while on the surface appearing different, is in actuality a very lonely existence. Other than the times I am speaking with the humans in my charge, I do not have the ability to interact with other beings that reside here. I'm separated from them, not because it is what is expected of me, but because in taking my job as seriously as I have, I have somehow managed to cut myself off completely from them.

Each day is spent going through the same motions, reaching out to a human or two, connecting with them on a level that they are inexperienced with and guiding them slowly but surely back toward the light they are destined for. It makes conversation with others like me, or even other angels, difficult to say the least. Any time spent away from the task at hand could spell disaster and that is something I am not willing to deal with.

Father placed his trust in me and I never want to do anything to break that. What is a little loneliness when placed side by side with the trust of the Almighty?

Chapter Two

Michael

I have never been happier to be home.

Despite what some would have you believe, doing as I have done today, no matter how many times I have been in the exact situation before, it never gets easier. It is in moments such as the one I find myself now, coming home again, that I wish for simpler times.

It was not always this way. There was a time where going on these missions for Father did not drain me as they do now. In fact, I found myself exhilarated by them. In completing something such as what I have just done and come back from, I felt satisfied and more than that, more alive than ever before.

I do believe things changed when I was tasked with removing Lucifer from Heaven. Where we used to go on these missions as a unit, now they were being split up and we were tackling them on our own, with no support from the beings we know as brothers. Going through all of this now, alone no less is extremely trying on me, but I will not back down despite the lingering feeling inside of me to do so. I will continue moving onward as Father expects of me because it is what I have been made to do.

When Father asked me to stand beside him, watching over both Heaven and what he created below, I had been honored. It was a place previously reserved for Lucifer and with him gone, it stood to reason the spot needed to be filled by a warrior of his caliber. I never imagined that it would be me, but there can be no mistaking that since I have been placed in the position, I have made it my own.

There is no celestial in existence more loyal to our father and what he wishes for the world than me.

It is only in doing what I have done today that my level of loyalty comes into play. It is never easy to face down one of your own, list their crimes against the light and Father, then rid the world of them, essentially making them cease to exist. I have done it on numerous occasions, both with my brothers by my side and alone, but each and every time it is as if a part of me ceases to exist with them.

That is not to say I feel for them. They would not be on the receiving end of my sword if they had not gone against what Father believes in, but they are still my family, regardless of what they have believed in or done and it is that way of being that makes what I must do so difficult. It is an experience that leaves me drained and longing for nothing but solitude in order to bring myself back to where I need to be to serve Father again.

He has been preoccupied lately, our father. After spending a great deal of time focusing his attention on creating the most magnificent ball of light, the time has come for it to be sent down into the world below. It is this ball of light that is meant to change the world, but only when the time is right. Father is the only one that knows when the right time is, but his focus, all of his light, has been pushed solely into this particular undertaking, which leaves the rest of us to pick up the slack.

Due to my position by his side, I am to be a part of this undertaking, but until such time as he calls for me in that regard, I must continue on as I have been. That means taking care of angels that should have fallen with Lucifer, but who still remain in Heaven, wreaking their particular brand of havoc and attempting to do so undetected. It is that which I am returning from now.

Samael, an angel of the highest order. One that until the moment I plunged my sword deep into the recesses of his chest, I had called brother without conviction. Samael and Lucifer had been close at one time, but after my older brother had been removed and fallen to the earth below, it appeared as though Samael had chosen the right path once more and had been prepared to tow the line.

We were mistaken and it cost us. Beings of light, ones that had not quite earned their wings, but were surrounded by the heavenly light had been massacred and he had done much the same on the planet. Humans turned up dead and after ruling my fallen brother out as well as the demons he employed, our attention turned to who resided here at home.

It is hard for my brothers to believe that a being born of such pure light, as we all are could be twisted so much that they create the destruction that Samael did. I have never been like them in that regard. I see things much the way Father does. All beings, whether good or evil in nature have the ability to be turned and though I did not see Samael being the one that did so, it was not all that surprising.

I had done as Father asked, Samael no longer exists and now that it has been taken care of, I am home again in order to surround myself with the light, love and acceptance that is present here. I am here to heal that which has been broken inside of me. I may be one of the strongest warriors, but that does not mean I am not without the ability to break. My form has been wounded, my heart slaughtered and the way it feels walking through the gates again, I know beyond a shadow of a doubt that I will be back to myself in no time at all.

"I was beginning to wonder if you would ever return."

"Loss of faith in my abilities already, Gabriel? You wound me."

"I assure you, there can be no doubt about your ability as a warrior, Michael. I merely meant that the mission Father sent you on, it was longer than expected."

He is not wrong. It had taken far longer than anyone could have foreseen handling Samael. Father had not expected it to be easy, nor did I, but what had taken a week on the planet below, was far longer here in Heaven. This might be one of the longest periods of time I have spent away from home in years.

"You know Samael as well as I do. He would not go willingly. He could not accept that his end was indeed what Father wanted. There was far more back and forth than I am used to."

"How long are you back for this time?"

If there is a brother that understands what it means to be a warrior for our Father, it is Gabriel. He is sent down to the planet far more than I am and he seems to enjoy his time there, but just like me, he has experienced missions such as the one I had regarding Samael and knows that there are more just like him around the bend.

"I am unsure how much time he will allow me to have. I know that I am tasked with accompanying the ball of light down to the planet any time now, so I think it won't be very long."

"Is it everything you imagined it would be when you said yes?"

He does not need to explain what he means. He is speaking of my saying yes to Father after Lucifer fell. It is no secret that the position was coveted by many here at home and the fact that I had been the one to end up with it, still did not sit right with many. Knowing what a perfect fit I am for it though, the question is a valid one.

"It is that and more Gabriel. I was made for this. While you seem to thrive when you are helping those in need below us, I cannot say the same. Standing by our father, taking in everything he does, being privy to all that he does not want to share with the majority, it is exhilarating and I do not regret it for a second."

"Do you ever wonder if you are meant for something more?"

"What is with all the questions little brother? What have you been told about that? It serves no one and will only hurt you in the long term."

I can see that my words have hurt him and it was not my intent, but there can be no denial of the truth. It began with

Lucifer much the same way and I would hate to see the same fate befall another brother. Gabriel is meant for so much more than Lucifer and he would be better off remembering that instead of asking questions and going against it.

"I am aware of what I have been told and what can happen to one that questions our father. I am merely asking because I am curious."

"I do not believe I am meant for anything more than this," I answer, unable to completely disregard his question. "Is that a good enough answer for you brother?"

"It is not as if there is a right or wrong answer to the question. As I said, I was merely curious." He answers before turning as the atmosphere around us shifts and we're no longer alone together.

"Gabriel, while I appreciate you being here to welcome your brother home, it is time for us to speak alone."

Father likes to have these moments after a difficult mission. In a way, I believe he does it so he keeps those of us he has chosen to bring close, pure of heart and mind so that we will not be tempted to follow in our brother's footsteps, but one can never truly tell.

Once Gabriel has taken his leave and we are alone together, he turns to me and the look on his face says all that his words can never say. He is bathed in the brightest light and he is smiling his approval. It is moments such as these that at one time, I enjoyed baring witness to, but after this mission, all that it took out of me, it is not what I am feeling at all.

Obliterating one of my own, especially Samael, never should have taken place, even if it was on Father's orders. I am aware that I have done the right thing, at least as far as Heaven goes, but there is something buried deep inside me that does not feel that I have done right at all. We need all the warriors and bringers of light that we can get our hands on in the upcoming battle that is sure to come with Lucifer. Ridding ourselves of one, especially one as powerful as Samael, well, there can be nothing right about that.

"My son, you have done Heaven a great service today, one that you will be rewarded for. What you experienced with Samael, I know could not have been easy, but in the long term know that you have turned things around in our favor. The light continues to live on in such a powerful way because of the steps you have taken today."

"How many more traitors am I going to have to come face to face with in this fight you have spoken of?"

"We will continue to eradicate those that should have been removed with Lucifer for as long as it takes to purify Heaven of the darkness your brother implanted."

So I will be doing this forever. Fantastic.

"Michael, I am aware that the battle with Samael took a lot out of you, but you must not think the way you are. As I have said, you did what was needed and you should be proud of that. We are doing what is needed to make all things right again."

"You make it sound so simple."

He is right. I do not normally behave in this manner. I proceed ahead doing what is needed of me, not questioning it or Father's reasoning behind it. As much as I do not want to admit to any form of weakness, the battle with my former brother did indeed bring about that very thing within me. I feel weaker than I ever have before.

"Gabriel asked a question of me earlier and I was unable to give him a proper answer."

"What question would that be?"

"How much time am I being given in order to heal from what I have just been through?"

"Samael, for all the darkness that grew inside of him was an integral part of Heaven and his loss will be felt for some time. In fact, I do believe it will take you far less time to heal from your physical wounds than it will to heal from the emotional implications of what has been done. You have as long as you need, Michael."

There is a moment when he is speaking that I want to stop him. Some of what he is saying is meant for my other brothers and not for me. When I was created, it was for one purpose. I was to be the strongest, mightiest warrior Heaven has ever seen. In doing so, it means that I am unlike my brothers before me. I do not feel as they do, so his talk of emotional implications is not needed here.

"Just because I made you to be a warrior does not mean you are devoid of all feeling, my son. At some point it would serve you greatly to embrace every facet of yourself and not just the ones you are most comfortable with."

"You did not choose me to stand by your side because of emotion, Father. You chose me because there could be no one better to stand by your side and offer what you need most moving ahead in the way you are."

"That may be, but what I previously stated remains true. A true warrior and one as pure as you, embraces all parts of himself; even the parts that he does not like."

I know better than to question the words of my creator, for he is known to speak nothing but the truth, but I cannot help myself. Can there be truth in his words? Is it possible that I am more than just a warrior and that it is acceptable for me to feel, especially now with what happened to Samael?

Emotion has never had a place in what I am. Showing emotion only opens you up so your weaknesses are exposed and until this moment in time, I believed that if everyone could see it that way, there would be far less pain present, both above and below.

"Michael, you must not allow your mind to be overloaded with thoughts such as this. Take some time, bathe yourself in the purity that being home brings and everything that is troubling you now, will seem like a distant memory."

Faith

As much as I love my job and cannot imagine doing anything else, it is in moments like the one I am bearing witness to that make me question if I am indeed the right person to do it.

The human I have been charged with watching over, he is struggling and despite his every attempt at remaining strong, the walls he has constructed are beginning to crack. My heart breaks for him and I want nothing more than to disobey the order and help him now instead of waiting until he has reached his breaking point.

There is an order here and it is one that I must follow to the letter. I am to interact with the humans that need me most, but not until there seems to be no other alternative. I must remain an observer until such time as it looks as though they are ready to meet their end and then intervene. It is the one part of the job that I do not like.

Being made of the light, originally a ball of energy that would possibly be used to save the world, I am more emotional than most that reside here. I feel things on a deeper level than even God himself and despite my every attempt to bury it in order to get the job done, I am not very good at it. My heart breaks for each individual I am charged with and the need to step in before the right time builds with each new assignment.

Colin McDougall is the human currently in my charge. His story appears the way a sad movie might. Where one would expect to see moments of happiness and delight, in his story there is no such thing. It started the day he was born. His mother was lost in childbirth. The way Father explained it to me, it was written that she would be lost and her soul returned home, but despite knowing that, it does not make it easier to take. From there, he remained with a father that abused alcohol and did nothing but hate for his entire childhood. It was during this point that I most wanted to intervene, but was not allowed to do it. When he turned sixteen, tragedy struck again as the abusive father took a gun and shot himself right in front of the boy.

Again I wanted to intervene, the horrors that the boy had been dealing with becoming too much for even a being of light to handle. After being taken from the home a week after the horrible incident, shuffled from home to home for three years, he ended up on his own. At first he lived on the street and then after a shopkeeper took a chance on him, he began living in an apartment above a restaurant. Where he seemed stable, at least for the time being, it was not to last. He found drugs shortly after and because of the hold they had on his life, he again ended up on the street.

He has almost been lost to us twice now. Both times from an attempted overdose. Whether or not he is attempting to take his own life or is just so addicted to the medication that he loses track of himself is unclear, but whatever the reason, he is in desperate need of saving. I have no doubt that if I do not step in soon, the next time this happens, it will be his last.

The first time he overdosed, I went to Father, assuming he would say it was time for me to reach out to the boy. If he was as near death as he appeared and it was not supposed to be his time, than surely I had to get involved. I was mistaken. Apparently, he had been expecting this very thing to happen and I was to follow along as always, watching but not becoming involved.

That is a thing not many know about, unless you are like me and reside here. Every human enters the earth with a chart. It has been written how their life will be lead and also how they will pass on when it is their time. The problem with this chart is, the only one that knows all that is contained in it is Father. I know of some things, but most of what I learn, I do so by watching the human. If I had any idea what was contained in a lot of the charts of the people I have saved, or even the ones I have lost, I might be able to do that much more in order to bring them back into the light in a much better way than I have been.

I am not afforded that luxury though. I must follow along as Father asks of me even if I do not like it. He knows how I feel and he has even sympathized with me at times because he knows what he instilled in me when I was created. He knows that I am the emotional bringer of light. I am the one that feels far more than an angel should and I am also the one that will stop at nothing in order to have a positive result. The one thing I do not do that sometimes I wonder if I should, is question things.

You do not question God. All you have to do is look at the fate afforded to Lucifer to know what questioning our father will accomplish. I do not want to end up like the original fallen angel, of that I am sure, but with all that has been spoken of as it pertains to my father, I would expect him to be more feeling and less action, but it is the complete opposite. As much as he loves, he does not show it nearly as much as he should.

Watching Colin as he struggles, there is an ache in my chest that even looking away from the boy cannot erase entirely. It is almost time for me to reach out to him, I can sense it, but I cannot help feeling that any attempt I make now will be for naught. It will have been too late in the game and he will become another casualty. As hard as I fight the doubts, it is impossible to erase them. I do not want to fail this boy.

"Faith, the time is upon us."

"Yes Father, I am aware. I am just not sure that anything I do now will be able to turn him off this path of self-destruction."

"He is not meant for Lucifer. You must trust in your ability to change the ending of his story."

"Is it not the ending you have said is meant to happen? I do not believe I will be changing anything at all."

"In a manner of speaking you are changing it. The path he finds himself on will only lead to darkness, despair and a life spent in the chambers of Hell. You reaching out to him can turn it all around. It is what you were made to do."

"I will do my best, but as I have said, we may have waited far too long with this particular human. The level of loss within him is painful."

"Then it is a good thing I have my most trusted bringer of light handling it."

He has always done this. When one loses faith in themselves, there is no being better equipped to bring them back to their rightful spot than Father. He is aware of my doubts regarding the boy and my own ability to save and heal him and he is letting me know that he believes in me. It is that faith, so to speak that pushes me forward where before I wanted to stop, much like the very human I am charged with taking care of.

"Reach out to the boy, Faith; as only you can. Bring him back into the light. Show him the way."

As quickly as he appeared before me, he vanishes and I am left alone with Colin. The first step with the boy is to wait until he is at his most relaxed, his mind clear, and then appear to him there.

What most do not realize is that being created of the light, it is often too much for humans to handle. That is not to say that there are not humans with abilities that make seeing us in true form much easier to take, but for the majority, doing so would cause far more grief then needed. It is why I always choose to enter through the mind first. They may not believe in what is happening, but it far easier to break through barriers when it's not staring you in the face.

I want nothing more than to save Colin McDougall. I want to bring him back into the light and make sure that for the remainder of his time on the planet, he enjoys his life. It is what Father wants most of all with the humans. Happiness. The more of that they experience, the more light takes over darkness and we become one step closer to winning the war we seem to be facing since Lucifer's banishment.

It is the time of night where he is at his most calm. I can feel the hatred, anger and darkness draining away as his eyes become heavy before my own. It is time for me to do as Father said and reach out to him. With one final look, taking in the damage he has spent the last two years doing to his body, I attempt to figure out the best way to begin.

As I am about to reach out to his mind, I hear it. A sound I had not been expecting as it is not something I have encountered with the boy in my earlier dealings with him. He appears to be sleeping but there is more to it. The magnitude of everything he has had to deal with has finally taken its toll and it has happened in a way I am most unfamiliar with.

Colin McDougall is crying, though it is blocked by his position in his pillow. It only makes the ache in my heart for him more difficult to handle. He deserves so much more than what he has been given. It is now the perfect time for me to prove it to him.

Hear the sound of my voice, Colin and allow your heart to calm.

As expected the muffled sound ceases and he moves upwards in his bed, his eyes darting around the room at an alarming speed. It is the response most expected when in a situation such as this and one I am more than equipped to handle.

"Who said that? What the hell is going on? Show yourself."

I would like nothing more than to present myself before you now Colin, but it is not the right time.

"Holy shit, I'm losing my mind. I need to stop taking shit before bed."

You should cease taking anything period, but until such time as you are strong enough, I do believe it would be wise that you cease all extracurricular activities before bed, yes."

"Who the hell are you and what do you want with me?"

For whatever reason, his mind is coming to terms with the fact that he is not able to see me, yet knows I am very real. I am sure he does not believe in the concept of higher beings, but his acceptance of my voice in his head pleases me. It means that the first step has been taken care of. I only hope I can keep the momentum going moving forward.

My name is Faith and I am here to watch over you. The pain you feel deep inside you, threatening to break you; I am here to make sure does not happen.

"Why do you give a shit? No one else does."

"I give a shit because you are meant for so much more. I know that it does not seem that way now, but if you just believe and hang in there, I will get you to the place you are meant to be."

"The only place I'm meant for is a pine box six feet under."

You are mistaken. You are meant to live a happy life, one filled with laughter, love and light.

"How the hell do you figure that? What do you know that I don't?"

I have knowledge of the way your life is meant to turn out. When the time is right, I can tell you more, but until such time as that happens, I need you to hold on just a little while longer.

"I don't want to be here anymore. I just want to die."

I know you do, but that is not going to happen today, or any day in the near future. I will not allow it. Please do not let the darkness win.

"What the hell do you know about darkness? You're just a random voice in my head for Christ's sakes."

I know more than enough about the darkness, but I know even more about the light. It is the very thing I am guided by. I am here to make sure that there is only that very light present in your life.

"And if I don't want it?"

This is a question I have gotten on more than one occasion but it never gets easier to answer. Most bound for a dark path do not want anything to do with the light or the second chance it can bring. It is up to me to make them see the reality of the situation and change their way of being. It will be more difficult with Colin because the question he asks, has never been asked of me this soon.

You are unsure of what you want right now, but I will not leave you until you do.

"Everybody leaves."

That may be your experience, but I am here to tell you it is not the case at all.

"Oh yeah? My mom went and died when she had me, my dad couldn't handle me so he shot himself, and every foster parent I had after that got rid of me faster than a person can blink. You wanna tell me again how you know that people actually stay?"

I know there are people that never leave because I am one of them. Colin, I am here for you and I am not going anywhere. I am with you always.

Chapter Three

Michael

Something monumental is happening, but for whatever reason, Father is choosing not to share it with me.

It started about two days after I came home from the situation with Samael. At first there was his strange behavior. Despite everything he deals with, his demeanor never changes. I would not go out of my way to say that he is jovial all the time, but there is a happiness about him that we only aspire to have. That is not the case these last few days. He seems off in some manner, but no matter how much time I spend with him, I am unable to ascertain just what that is.

I have been working diligently beside him despite his request that I take it easy. In the times where I heed his earlier advice to me, I watch him, learning all there is to know about the way Heaven operates and it is because of this that I have seen the changes.

He will not speak of it. The one conversation we had, he avoided all mention of what is going on with him, instead focusing on explaining to me that he needed my help and exactly what I would be expected to do. While I am happy with the level of trust he is placing in me, asking me to do what he has, it does not stop the craving inside of me to know more.

I have been tasked with guarding over Heaven while he heads to Earth. It appears that there is something going on there that needs his full attention. He has had no problem in the past sending me or one of my brothers down to handle things, but in this regard it is something so monumental that it can only be handled by him. Knowing what looms on the horizon as it pertains to the ball of light he has chosen, I can only assume it is something to do with that.

*****

"I am aware that you have just recently returned home and I was the one that said I did not want to put any undo strain on you as you acclimate back, but there is something I must discuss with you. It is of the utmost importance."

"Father, you can bring anything to me, you know this. What is it that you need of me?"

"What I need from you Michael, it is no small undertaking. Please think on it considerably before giving me your answer."

"There is no thought needed Father. What you need from me, I will do."

"While I admire how easily you answer me and the truth behind your words, please do as I have requested."

"Of course. What is it that you require of me?"

"There is a situation of sorts below and in the past, I have had no issue sending you or your brothers, but this time, I am afraid it has to be dealt with by me. What I need of you Michael, is to watch over Heaven in my absence."

For as long as I have existed, a moment like this has never taken place. Father has moved through various plains more times than I can count, but it was never for an amount of time that would require him to ask this of any of us. Whatever he has to deal with had to be of the utmost importance, of that I was sure.

"Are you sure that leaving Heaven in my command is the right move?"

"There is no one I trust more with this task, Michael."

I am honored to hear him speak of me in such high regard and even though he asked me to think over my response to his request, I find that I do not need to. It is exactly as I have said previously, I will do what is needed.

"You do not need to give me your answer now, as I do not have to leave quite yet, but please do think on it and let me know as soon as you have decided."

"Father, you already know my answer so there is no time needed in order to think things through. I would be honored to do this for you."

"Are you positive? You have not been back all that long and I am concerned it may be too much too soon."

"I find that I am not like the others. I do not enjoy my time on the planet nearly as much as Gabriel or even Uriel when he does go. I much rather enjoy overseeing things here, by your side. It is where I am most comfortable. So to answer your question, even though I do believe no answer is needed, I am more than positive about this."

"Things should be rather calm in my absence, which is why I need to handle this now, but should you run into any issues, do not hesitate to call for me."

That is a secret of Heaven that no one but my brothers are aware of. Father is all knowing, but when he goes to the planet and has to interact with the humans, taking a vessel, it is as if that ability is cut off in him. It is not gone entirely, but the vessel prevents him from being as all knowing and seeing as he is here. If anything did happen, I would have to communicate with him in a more traditional way.

"I will do whatever is needed in order for things to remain as you have made them, of that you can be assured, Father."

"Of that I have no doubt."

"I wish to ask you something as it pertains to your mission, but I do not want to disrespect you."

"You want to know what it is regarding, do you not?"

As I nod he smiles, but just like it's been since I returned home, it doesn't reach all the way through him as it does normally. There is most definitely something big in play here and it is causing him obvious discomfort.

"Yes. I wish to know so that I can help you."

"The way you can help me most is to take care of things here while I am gone. I want to say more, but if I speak of this openly, I am afraid it will alter what has been written and you know that is not a chance I am willing to take."

I have to accept his words even though there is a small part of me dying to question him for more. He trusts me with a task that he has never allowed of anyone, both before and after Lucifer had been removed and questioning him now would only mar the gift he was giving so freely.

"I will do as you need, Father. I will not let you down."

*****

It occurred to me shortly after that conversation that it may not have anything to do with the ball of light at all and with Lucifer himself, but with everything he said about being unable to tell me, I was not about to push my luck and ask again. It is hard to do though when you watch your father virtually changing before your eyes.

There is no light more magnificent than his, but now as he stands beside me, it seems duller than usual. Almost as if his thought process, what we are not privy to is hurting him in some way. He is not an unfeeling being the way he has been portrayed in texts, but he is not quite as emotional as Gabriel. What I see now, speaks to him feeling a lot more than he cares to admit and it is dimming his very light. I need to get him to speak of this, if only to ease the ache in my own heart at seeing him this way.

It is the only time that I am aware of, other than my momentary lapse with Samael that I have felt anything at all. When it pertains to the creator of all things, emotion cannot be seen as wrong. In order for things to remain as beautiful as they are here, his well-being has to matter and it is that very thing I am focused on so strongly now. I need to be sure that he is okay.

"Father, I have not wanted to mention this, but the last few days together, you do not seem like yourself."

"I am aware of the changes you are witnessing, Michael. You have no reason to fear bringing it to my attention."

"Does it have something to do with what you are about to face?"

"It does."

"I know you have said you do not want to change that which has been written, but maybe in this one instance, it is what is needed."

"I cannot argue with your logic, but I will not speak of it. In a few short hours, you will be left here to guard over Heaven while I head down to the planet. I want to be sure moving forward that you are sure in your choice to do this."

There is my father. He is changing the subject much like the humans do when they are feeling most uncomfortable. In putting the focus on me, he can take it off himself and hopefully divert my attention to other pursuits. It is a tactic that I can see working on the other beings here, but he has to realize by now that I will not be so easily swayed.

"As I have told you, I will do what is needed of me and do it without question. You can be secure in the knowledge that things will carry on as they have been thus far. You will come back from your trip and take the reins back without fear of what has happened in your absence."

"It is hard to believe that only a few short days ago, you were questioning whether or not you were up to the task, or rather that you were the right choice. It is as if I am speaking with a whole new Michael."

"You did say that I needed time to recuperate, did you not? I am sure that the last few days have given me all that I need so that I can do that which you have asked of me."

"It appears to be that way, but please concern yourself not with what I am about to face as I head down to Earth, but only what happens here. I will be fine, of that you can be assured."

There is so much truth mixed into his words that I cannot doubt him, but it does not calm the voice inside of me that wants to know exactly what it is he will be facing.

"Does this have anything to do with Lucifer?"

"It does not and with that I have already said too much. Trust in me, Michael."

"I trust you implicitly."

"Then free your mind of the questions and use the remainder of our time together to make sure everything is as it needs to be. All will be revealed in time, I assure you."

Faith

This particular human is proving to be more difficult than I imagined.

I have come to him, each day for the past three human days and every visit is much the same. I cannot seem to break through his walls. I only need one small instance of the light, some form of acceptance inside him and I will be able to bring him back to where he needs to be, but with each passing day, I am beginning to doubt it even exists.

Going to Father crossed my mind after the second day, but I thought better of it. If he didn't believe in my ability to do my job, he would never have given it to me in the first place. My track record with the humans in this way has proven what an asset I am. The last thing I want is to go to him because one human seems to be harder than most. It would surely tear apart everything I have worked so hard for.

Colin has told me to go away more times than I can count, going so far as to get annoyed with me when I do not do as he asks. The first few times he said it, I would break away from him, believing that in giving him the time he was desperately asking for, he would come to realize how important having me with him was, but that never happened. I came back after that and I have not left since.

His human heart remains beating in his chest and that is a victory in its own right, but I want more than that. I want to be able to break through his barriers and bring him back into the light where he belongs. I just wish I could tell him that.

We are permitted to go to them though it is not advised, but we are not permitted to tell them exactly who we are and the real reason for us being there. We can give details, the way I did the first day, in telling him that he was to live quite longer than he assumed, but more than that and it would be considered breaking the rules. That is something I cannot afford to do, even though I want nothing more than to give him the absolute truth.

I've wanted to do that with every human I have come across. I attach myself to them in such a way that when they are low, I feel low and vice versa. We are connected even though they know nothing of who I really am and what I have been sent to do. At least they are unaware until they have been brought back into the light. That is the point at which I am able to tell them exactly who I am and what my purpose for annoying them as often as I did really is.

For so long, I believed myself to be alone in the annoyance I feel at having to hide who I am from the humans I am trying to help, but it appears I am not as alone as I thought. Over the last couple of days, I have been visited by one of the highest ranking angels in Heaven and he has bared witness firsthand to the struggle I am having with Colin. It is from his visit that I am able to see that there are others out there that feel just as I do and that we want the same things in the end, even if that ending goes against all that our Father has put forth.

Gabriel.

It is unbelievable to me that an angel of his caliber would visit me, let alone become involved in any way with what I am currently dealing with. Yet that is exactly what has taken place. He has taken time away from whatever he has been tasked with and spent time watching over Colin with me, offering advice as an outsider and I find the more time he spends here, the more I learn how alike we really are.

He feels just as I do. He has what the humans call, a big, soft heart and he is not against using it in any given situation. After all of my dealings with Father and the other angels with their never wavering attitude in dealing with things, it is such a refreshing change to see someone like him. It is my first experience with an archangel and I am thankful that the one I did get to interact with the first time is him.

"You have seen the way he is. What do you suggest I do in order to break through?"

"That is a difficult question to answer. The level of pain inside of him, I have never seen anything quite like it. Are you sure that Lucifer has not already marked him?"

"I am quite sure it hasn't happened yet. You know as well as I do that he would not interact with me at all if Lucifer marked him. I fear that it is not far off though, if he continues down this road."

"Have you ever encountered a being quite like him before?"

"No. There have been difficult cases in the past and a couple of them have even been lost to the darkness, but nothing this extreme this early."

"May I offer you some advice?"

"Of course."

"Keep trying, at least for a few more days. If you cannot seem to break through or if things begin to happen that you cannot stop on your own, call for me."

"You seem eager to help. Why is that?"

"It has been quite some time since I have interacted with the humans. I feel as though lately, I am drifting in a sea of nothingness. Helping you, given that there is nothing for me to do otherwise would please me greatly."

I have been interacting with him easily over the last little while, yet he still finds ways to amaze me. I always assumed that my first interaction with a being of his caliber would end badly, given the way I am in regard to my feelings and emotional displays, but with Gabriel, it is as if my way of being is accepted.

"That is because it is accepted. Despite what you have been shown here since your creation, we are not all uncaring and unfeeling. Some of us feel far too much for our own good."

His mouth curves up into a smile and I cannot help but return it with one of my own. Before Gabriel had come to watch over me, I had been doing just as he said. I was drifting and again, the way it had with Father before, it felt as though I could not do anything right. He restored my strength and faith in my own abilities.

"We will sort this young man out, Faith. Never lose faith in your ability to change lives, make them better. I fear that if you do, then Heaven would lose one of the good ones and that would be a shame."

Chapter Four

Michael

"Brother, we need to speak."

Father has only been gone for a few days and already there is something that needs my attention. I can hear it in his tone. Gabriel would not come to me unless it was a matter of the utmost importance.

Whatever brings him to me now, he feels as though it is a life or death situation. It is not something I take lightly. I only hope that I am able to help him in the way Father would have.

"What is it, Gabriel?"

"There is a situation. At first I believed I would be able to handle it, but it appears as though even a being of my caliber is ill equipped for the task. I do believe that the only one capable of handling this is you."

"Well, do not keep me in suspense. What is this situation you speak of?"

"It is a human watched over by a bringer of light. I know that you do not have any communication with them, so you are unaware of what they even do, but I do believe once I explain the situation, you will want to help."

He is correct in his assumption. I do not know much of the bringers of light. All that I have been made aware of has come from Father and it has not been much. I do know they were all balls of light, created for the task at which only one could be chosen. Father had taken all of the others and placed them in various locations throughout Heaven, dealing with the humans that were considered tough cases. Humans that with just the right amount of motivation could become pawns in Lucifer's game.

"In what way am I able to help that you are not? You are the angel that primarily deals with the humans. What can I offer?"

"Your strength. I am aware that I am the angel that is primarily called on for this sort of thing, but brother, you have not encountered the human that we have. He is by far the toughest case I have ever come across."

"I do believe you need to tell me more as it pertains to the human and better yet, how you have come to know of it. Are you fraternizing with the bringers of light in your down time?"

"Do not make light of this, Michael. This is not a time for jokes. I sensed a struggle with Faith and when I came upon the situation, I tried as much as I could to help her. I am unable to do that any longer, which is where you come in."

"I am listening. Start from the beginning and tell me everything you know."

"It would be easier to just show you."

"For now, just do as I ask, Gabriel. For once do not question it. Tell me so that I can decide where to go from there."

"As I told you, I came across Faith, noticed the struggle she was having with her current charge and intervened, but it appears as though even with the power I possess, I am unable to break through."

"Tell me about the human."

"His name is Colin McDougall, he is a young adult. There is nothing particularly extraordinary about him, but he seems to be able to fend off intervention without much effort. I will spare you the emotional end of things, but he has not had the easiest life and because of that, he finds himself reaching the point of no return quicker than most."

The way Gabriel explains everything to me, leaving out the emotional aspects bothers me. I am aware that he is doing it to save time, but is it really how I appear to him? When I asked for all the information, I meant it. Even the parts of it that I might not identify with. It is no secret that I do not handle emotions well, but it does not mean I am not interested in knowing.

In order to help the boy as my brother requires, it is those very parts I am going to know the most about. If he is this close to the darkness than it is emotionally driven and if we are to save his life we have got to use those parts to our advantage.

"I appreciate your need to want to keep things simple, but you must inform me of everything, even if it is something I have limited familiarity with."

"He is suicidal, Michael. I am sure you have lived long enough to know what that entails so I do not need to go into detail. Yes, it is as you suspect. This is emotionally driven. He has nothing left to live for and the longer he believes that, the closer he is to becoming Lucifer's pawn."

"It was not all that long ago that you sympathized with Lucifer, so why are you so concerned with whether or not we lose this particular human to him?"

"It is not the way that it has been written. I would have thought that was obvious, but more than that, there is a light inside of him. We just need to reignite it."

"How do you propose I do that when the means at which you have tried have failed?"

"Maybe I am not able to break through because I am too close to the situation, much the same way that Faith is. I am willing to concede that maybe, this time, we need an outsider point of view."

I am aware of what he means by outsider perspective. Because of the way I appear to beings that reside here, my lack of attachments and my ability to stay level when anyone else would show some form of emotion, I am their last hope. They want to use me because I am cold.

"I do not believe you to be cold, Michael, but yes, you are correct in the reason I bring this to you instead of going to Raphael or Uriel. You are far more level headed and right now, I do believe that is what the boy needs."

"Well, what are we waiting for? If I am to help in the manner that you and the bringer of light need, then we need to work fast."

"You are going to help?"

"I do believe that is what I said brother. It would serve you better to keep up. Take me to the bringer of light. It is time that I meet her and find out all the avenues she has tried thus far. I will not move forward with this until I have been informed of everything."

It is in the moment that I see the smile spread across my brother's face, the light surrounding him brightening that I realize that there is something more going on with Gabriel than just his concern for the human. For whatever reason, the idea of me standing before the bringer of light appeals to him and I am most annoyed by it.

What is he aware of that I am not and just what is taking this on while Father is away going to cost me in the end?

Chapter Five

Faith

When Gabriel left earlier, I was not expecting him to ever come back. It was not in his job description to watch over me or to even go so far as to give me a pep talk in order to keep me focused on my task. He had done all of that of course, but it did not change the facts. He had much more important things that he needed to be doing.

When he appeared before me again, not long after he left though, I started to get another view of what this particular archangel is all about. He is not quite like the others. In a way, he is somehow better, though I would never go so far as to tell him that. All of the archangels were made as equals and to appreciate one more than another was forbidden.

It is well known in Heaven that Michael, Raphael, Uriel and Gabriel work hand in hand with Father and the missions and undertakings that they oversee are of the utmost importance. To see an angel of Gabriel's caliber willing to break protocol and help a lower level being, was probably the most shocking thing I have come across in my short time here.

"I do believe I have found a way to help the boy, but it is not going to be something you want to hear."

"At this point I am willing to accept any form of help afforded to me."

"You might not feel that way when I have told you everything."

I know that they do not interact with us often, but surely he must know that I mean what I say. I would not have uttered the words at all otherwise. It is not the way I operate.

"Faith, there is never a lack of entertainment when I spend time with you. The way in which you think; it is refreshing and completely unnecessary. I know that you are speaking the truth. I just fear that once you had heard all that I have to say, you will not agree with the lengths I have gone to."

"Well there is only one way to find out."

He smiles and there is something comforting about it. It is not at all what I would have thought I would feel when in the presence of someone like him. If the stories that have been spoken about them are true, the very last thing anyone feels when in their company is comfort.

"Do you always get to the point in this way?"

"You mean to tell me there is any other way to be?"

"That is a good point. You also seem to make a lot of those."

"It would appear to be that way. I mean no disrespect by it, I assure you."

He tips his head almost as if he is confused by the way I am reacting and the comfort of earlier fades away as I become filled with dread. Having no interaction before with the archangels, I am unsure of how to even approach one of them, let alone how to act once they have been in my company far longer than just the one instance.

"Faith, you must realize something about me. I am not like my brothers. You will do nothing to offend me in any way. I do not bruise as easily as you think. I rather like my time with you. You remind me of someone."

"Who is it that I remind you of?"

"You, bringer of light will learn of that sooner than you think."

Well, that was vague.

"After leaving you earlier," Gabriel states, changing the subject and bringing us back to what should have been most important all along. Colin. "I decided to try a different tactic as it pertains to your charge."

"And that would be?"

"As you are aware, Father has taken a vessel and left Heaven for an undetermined amount of time. In his absence, Michael has been put in charge. I have taken the situation to him."

Leaving me, he had taken it to his brother? Not only his brother, but one of the strongest angels in Heaven? Did something as trivial as this even register on his radar?

"You have every right to ask those questions. What seems to be important to you and me, is not the same for Michael, or even my other brothers. At this point though, with me unable to help you in the manner you need, he is the only option we have."

"May I ask you something?"

"You can ask me anything, at any time Faith. What is it you wish to know?"

"Going to Michael, is that what you think I will be unhappy with?"

"You catch on quickly."

I do not have the heart to tell him that he had already given himself away when he arrived. If there was more to know about the steps he had taken, he was not getting to them in a timely manner, so it was only natural that I jump to that conclusion.

"What makes you think Michael will help us? If he is overseeing Heaven the way you say, surely he has far more pressing issues on his plate."

"You do not know my brother. What he has taken on recently, he was born to do and he handles himself flawlessly. As one of our kind should."

"Now that we have gotten that out of the way, how is it exactly that you expect him to help?"

"That is the other thing that I need to speak with you about."

He had my attention now. Not only had he called on his brother to help us, which I was more than grateful for, but he was most forthcoming about it. Almost as if he did not want anything hidden between us.

"Michael wishes to speak with you regarding all that you have done in an effort to help the human."

"I do not see the problem, Gabriel."

"There is no problem, but I feel that I need to warn you before he arrives. My brother, he is not like I am. He is like no other being in creation. I am afraid that when he does arrive, you will not feel comfortable in his company."

"You act as though you have invited Lucifer to tea! I assure you, I can handle your brother, no matter what way he appears when he arrives."

"I do believe the angel has let her ego get the better of her."

It is only when I look to Gabriel and see his form standing straighter, more rigid even, that I realize it had not been him that had spoken the words, but the very angel we had just been in discussion about.

Based on his first words spoken, I know Gabriel had spoken the truth. Michael was nothing like the other archangel standing before me now, and the smug look I am met with as I take him completely in, brings to the surface an urge deep inside of me to slap it off of him.

It is time to meet Michael and despite his claim about my ego, there is no way I am going to let him run all over me. He can hear me out and choose to help or he could move on. He might be one of the most powerful beings in Heaven, but that did not mean I had to take attitude during his time with me.

In fact, I wouldn't be the one taking attitude at all. He would.

Michael

It is not like me to notice such things, but the minute I touch down and hear the conversation between my brother and the bringer of light, I can't help but take it all in, starting first with their words and ending with a full view of exactly who I will be dealing with from here on out.

Gabriel is unaware of it, but after he left me and made his way back here in an effort to prepare her for my arrival, I did a lot of thinking about what avenue to take as it pertained to the broken boy. With Father signaling to me only a few short hours ago of his return, it made the plan I mapped out moving forward, easier to bring to life.

Once I have garnered all the information that I require regarding Colin and what has been done before my involvement, I do believe the best course of action moving forward is for me to make my way down to where the boy resides and help him in a human capacity.

I do not enjoy taking vessels. I loathe it almost as much as I do going to the planet as a whole, but in this regard, Gabriel having gone against his natural way of being and bringing this to me to begin with, I do believe it is called for. I must get over my hatred for all things human related and prepare myself for what I will encounter the minute I reach my destination.

Letting the bringer of light know that she would not be making the trek with me though, is a whole other situation in itself. It is her duty to be with the boy at all times and asking her to remain here while I go down and become involved in her task, is sure to upset her. It is what must be done and I have no doubt that when I am through with her, she will see it my way.

With our limited interaction with bringers of light, it comes as a surprise to me, the way she appears. Her face may now wear a scowl, but there can be no denial of the pure beauty underneath it all. She is a vision standing before me, even if she is experiencing momentary upset at my unexpected words and arrival.

"Michael, do you get some form of enjoyment from popping in this way?"

"I was unaware that we lived like the humans, brother. Should I have created an imaginary door and knocked on it to signal my arrival?"

"Somehow I doubt that you would ever do something respectable like that."

I have to hand it to the angel. She has a lot of gumption saying those things to me. With as much power as I command, especially with Father not here, she has to know the risks about turning on the very hand that feeds her.

"The only person that I have to answer to is *our* Father."

"If I had known that bringers of light had this kind of attitude, I would have popped in for a visit far sooner. Gabriel, just what have you gotten yourself into with this one?"

There has been a change in the atmosphere since I arrived and while I have done my best to ignore it over the last few minutes, it is harder to ignore watching the two of them now. They are close. I am unsure what about it upsets me, but there can be no mistaking the pain in my chest at watching my younger brother bond with another being of light.

Her attitude toward me intrigues me, so pushing the pain I feel away, something I am most proficient in, I focus on her and what it is about me that she loathes so much.

"I come here in order to help you at my brother's request and the minute I appear, you surround me with nothing but attitude. If Father knew of this, you are aware that he would not be pleased."

I had hoped my words would put her in some kind of place, where she would remember her role in the hierarchy of Heaven and back down, but as her stance goes even more rigid, I realize that is not going to be the case at all. This being is far stronger than I originally gave her credit for.

It pleases me to no end.

"If you are doing this for Gabriel, than one would think you would have appeared in a more appropriate manner instead of sneaking in and interrupting what was a private conversation."

"Silly girl, nothing is private here."

"Where you are concerned it is."

"Alright, the two of you stop it now! We are not here to argue back and forth. We are all on the same team. We need to come up with a way to help Colin McDougall."

This is the time where I need to speak up and state what I have decided. Inform them of my plans so that they will know their place and do as I have asked. I do not speak up though because I am too interested in hearing what the angel thinks. It appears as though even my body is betraying me as I am now standing aligned in her direction.

It is something I do not understand, nor like. Why am I reacting in this manner and with a bringer of light no less? Healers of the human heart is all they are and it is all they will ever be.

"Michael, that is completely inappropriate. I ask that you refrain from thinking such things if you want to do as I have asked."

There is one thing about Gabriel that has not changed since our creation. He may question Father and his actions or struggle with his need for constant information, but the one thing he does not do is speak to any of us the way he is now. Not only has he stepped inside my mind, abusing his ability to read my thoughts, but he has made mention of it openly. I am not pleased. This is not the Gabriel I know.

It appears as though the crush on the bringer of light has changed him, which is unacceptable.

"Stay out of my head, brother. I will not tell you nicely the next time it happens."

"I am not in your head. You are thinking so loudly that I am sure even Faith has heard you."

I cast a look toward the angel, again taking her in when I see no sign of her knowing what it is we are speaking of, I turn back to my brother and level him with a look that hopefully gets him to back down.

"Whatever the reason, please refrain from speaking openly of that which I am thinking. It does not have anything to do with the current company."

"Healer of human hearts is all she is? You believe that has nothing to do with her?"

This topic of conversation is getting us nowhere and judging by the pained expression across her face now, I can tell it has not made her happy. The annoying pain in my chest is back at seeing the way I have offended her and I do not enjoy it. I am an archangel, one of Father's most trusted and fierce warriors. The last thing I need to be concerned with is a look of displeasure on a lower level angels face.

"Is that what you really think of me and others like me?"

"Are you going to tell me that you are more than what you appear to be?"

"You know nothing about any of us. Having spent little to no time around anyone that does not reach your level of strength and power, how could you?"

"Control your girlfriend Gabriel, before I do it for you."

"That is ENOUGH, Michael!"

The way Gabriel's voice raises, his eyes turning to stone, I know I have hit a nerve, which I suppose was my intent all along. We need to get back on task here or this is just going to grow uglier by the second. The last thing I want is for Father to come home to all of us fighting.

"Fine. I'm sorry. It was not my intent to act this way. I am here now, so I suggest we get down to business."

As I wait for one of them to speak, I watch as Faith reaches out and her light connects to Gabriel's as she rests her hand on his arm. It is obvious she is doing it in order to calm him after his outburst, but witnessing it firsthand, does nothing to help my obvious tension at being here at all.

I do not want her touching him this way, it is far too intimate.

"Michael is right, we need to focus on Colin." She answers, finally backing away from my brother and her light again her own. A move that is not lost on me as everything appears to be normal again for me, the irritation at seeing them that close fading away at a rapid pace.

"Have you decided what course of action to take brother?" Gabriel asks, his eyes lingering anywhere but on me, his upset at my comment still clearly evident as his tone is shaky.

"Yes."

"Would you care to share with the rest of us?"

"I do believe it is time I found myself a vessel. I will need one if I plan on saving him."

Chapter Six

Faith

I have never been so infuriated in my life.

When Gabriel explained to me what he had done, I could barely hide my excitement. Sure, I knew that being in the presence of another archangel, one that even Gabriel himself said was most unlike him would be a daunting experience, but I was excited at the prospect of having help with Colin. It meant good things. Surely the more people involved in this undertaking meant that its odds went up for a better result.

It's no secret that I have been doubting my ability to do my job effectively, especially now that I seem to have a human I cannot break through to, but to have someone come in and basically say that what I did here means nothing, there is no way I am accepting that.

I know my place and I had not lied with what I said to the elder archangel. I did not answer to him and if he continues acting the way he is, then I would not allow him to be a part of this at all. It is my task to handle and I would not let anything interfere with it. Even someone with more power in his fingertips then I have in my entire form.

When he first appeared, I felt a change in the air, but had been so caught up with Gabriel that I had not given it a moment's notice. What I experienced upon his arrival, is something that I have never come into contact before, yet something I could easily discard. Maybe if I had paid more attention, he would not have gotten the chance to say the awful things that he has since being here.

I do not understand how two beings can be called brothers, yet be so different. It is not that I believe siblings must act the same. I have experienced enough humans over time to realize that everyone is an individual, but for them to be this far apart from one another, right down to the color of their light, was disconcerting. How can I go from being around a being such as Gabriel one minute and being dealt the angel that is Michael in another? Had Father created them this way on purpose?

Anger is not an emotion often displayed here. Sure, we have disagreements when things do not happen the way they have been written to, and there can be a backlash of emotion because of it, but it is unheard of for an angel to truly get angry. It is something reserved for Lucifer and the army he commands, but in coming across Michael the way that I have, anger is an emotion I am definitely feeling.

It might have something to do with the way my light seems to react when confronted with his, but the only thing clear is, I do not want any part of it. I am not anxious to experience anger in my existence, let alone have it directed toward another being of light. To turn away from him, his words and the obvious annoyance that is flowing through him at even being here at all though, would do far more damage than good.

I need him, or rather, we need him. If for any reason I step too far out of line and he turns away from this altogether, I know without question that we will lose Colin to the darkness. That is something I am not prepared to do. I must put whatever feelings I have toward the elder archangel in the background and focus strictly on what comes next in order to save the broken boy buried inside the destroyed man.

Having never come into contact with them before, the way he appears takes me aback. He stands mighty with a golden glow around him, but buried underneath the magnificent light is a being that looks nothing at all like his brother. Where Gabriel seems to employ a darker shade of long golden hair, Michael is the opposite. Standing tall, well above me, is a celestial that is blonde, but a lighter shade, and eyes, that even through the golden hue of the light come through an icy blue.

As much as he annoys me, getting under my skin like no other angel before him, there can be no denial of his purity. He is quite the beautiful specimen and I can see shades of our father within him.

He is not aware of it, but I saw the way he reacted to me reaching out to his brother. The minute my light connected to Gabriel's, there was a flash in his eyes I have never seen before and it did strange things to me. Seeing him react in the manner he did, hurt my soul and it is most confusing as to why that is happening at all. Before today I had never even met the angel, let alone interacted with him, so any reaction I have to him seems unwarranted. It should not be happening at all.

What would this mean working with him in the future? Would I be able to focus on the task at hand or would my consistent reactions to all he seems to do cause things to break down before they have even begun?

Faith, please free your mind of worry. It is time we hear Michael out. Everything else can be handled at a later date.

Before I can respond to the voice that I can clearly hear reverberating throughout my entire astral body, I hear the same voice speak aloud, this time louder than it had been seconds before, but putting me at ease. As long as I am here with Gabriel, dealing with Michael could indeed be handled easily. It was when we were separated that I was concerned about.

"You wish for us to go down to the boy?"

Michael is not as bad as he appears. It would seem that for you he feels the need to come off as what the humans like to call 'badass'. Pay him no mind.

"Gabriel, you think you're being cute speaking to her that way. You're not. Refrain from doing so. She is not one of your projects."

"For someone who does not feel nor care, you seem awfully touchy right now."

"You said that you want to go down to him." I interrupt, not wanting to hear the brothers get into it again. "What do you believe that will accomplish?"

"I am not sure it will accomplish much of anything, but until I spend some time with you and learn all that you have tried, I am going to go on the assumption that I appear before him in a way he can most accept and save his life that way."

"What exactly do you want to know?"

"The methods you have tried in order to reach out to him and aside from that, everything you can tell me about his existence up until this point. As my brother pointed out, I am the uncaring and unfeeling brother, therefore I cannot sympathize, but I can put on a show that appears as though I do when needed."

I cannot believe what I'm hearing. He wants to go down to Colin and pretend to care about him and his well being. What kind of angel is he? Sure, he might not feel and experience things the way I do, but does he really have to act as though he does? Are we not supposed to be honest beings above all else?

"You have spent far too long locked away here, Faith. This is why I do not want to deal with bringers of light. They know nothing of the reality of the situation because they have not seen the way the world can hurt the humans that inhabit it firsthand."

"Like you're so knowledgeable! I know a lot more about you than you think I do Michael. You spend every waking moment with our father. What could you possibly know about what Colin is experiencing?"

"Watch your tone with me, angel. Have you forgotten who you currently have to answer to? You would be smart to remember exactly who I am."

"You are bringing it on yourself brother. You are acting like a petulant child. Can you really blame her for reacting in this way?"

"Gabriel, I do believe you should be concerned about exactly what you are doing being involved with a bringer of light this way and less about my attitude."

"Can you both stop talking about me like I'm not even here? God, it's driving me crazy!"

Both men choose the minute I snap at them to finally back down from one another. I do not think so much of myself that I believe they are following my command, but I cannot help being happy that the fighting might finally end.

"You both came to me for my help. How I go about doing what needs to be done does not need to be any concern of yours. All you need to do is give me what I require in order to move forward."

"Who says you're moving forward alone?"

I cannot believe this guy. I understand who he is and I know what going against him would mean, but with the way he thinks so highly of himself, I feel the need to bring him down a few notches. Heaven is supposed to be a place of equality even if there is a hierarchy, but with the way he sounds now, he believes himself to be better than everyone else and it's annoying me to no end.

"Have you attempted to step into my mind as well?"

"No. All I have done since the moment you appeared is pay attention to the words you say. Everything is singular, almost as if you believe that once you get answers from me, you are handling all of this on your own."

"You are a quicker study then I first believed, Faith. You are picking up on that because it is indeed what will happen the minute I get what I need from you."

"Anyone ever tell you that you're a jerk?"

"That happens more than you know, Faith." Gabriel answers, a slim smile appearing over his face.

"What I am is not of consequence here. What is important is the well-being of the boy in your charge. If you did not want me to step in and take over, why bother coming at all?"

"I didn't come to you. He did." I answer easily, pointing to Gabriel, but not breaking eye contact at all with the stubborn angel before me. He is not going to win with me, despite his best attempts to do so. If he thinks he is the most stubborn being in Heaven, he was going to be in for a rude awakening.

I will not back down on this.

"Right and because he came to me, I am going to do what is necessary. You can run point from here, working whatever magic it is you beings work and I will go down and do what needs to be done directly with the boy."

"You will do no such thing!"

I am shouting and I know that it is the wrong move as Michael's entire body seems to tense at the sound, but there is no way he is setting this in stone. He might be in charge until Father gets back, but he is not God, no matter how much he wants to be.

"I assure you, Faith, this is not a power play or me having a God complex. This is all common sense. I suggest you follow along like a good angel so that we can resolve this quickly. Now, tell me what it is I need to know."

"I'm not telling you anything."

"Gabriel, can you please inform your girlfriend what she is doing going up against me in this way?"

"I'm not telling her anything. She is right. Her place is down there with you. That is what is needed. Going down on your own and leaving her here to watch is not the way Father would want things."

If I did not already respect and care for Gabriel the way I do, in this moment as he comes to my defense would surely do it. There is no way that Michael doing things his way is right and I do not care if it takes days, months or years, he is not leaving Heaven until he sees it.

"And if I never see it?"

"Then Colin will be lost, I will have to explain why to Father and things will surely become much more complicated than they need to be around here."

Unsure if what I'm seeing is even happening or just my wish coming true, Michael's eyes lower and the color within them darkens as his expression softens. There must have been something in what I said that got through to him. All I know is I am thankful for it. The tension surrounding the three of us has been suffocating for far too long.

"Than what, pre-tell do you suggest we do?"

"If you are going down to him, then I'm going too. We will save him together."

Chapter Seven

Michael

This is not going at all the way I want it to.

It was supposed to be a relatively easy fix. I would garner all the information I could about the boy from Faith and then I would head the planet and do everything in my power to heal him once Father returns. That is not at all the way it happened and there is nothing I can do.

The issue here is that it is not just me against her. If that had been the case, getting my way would have been easier, but she also has Gabriel on her side and if pushed, I have no doubt he will go to Father about this and I may never be trusted to look over Heaven in his absence again. I cannot afford to let that happen.

This angel infuriates me like no other before her. This is why I do not go out of my way to interact with the other beings of light that reside here. They consider us all equal and in the end cause more trouble than they are worth. The reason she bothers me so much, it's not one particular thing she's done. It is because she is right and I cannot stand it.

She is the boy's keeper. I may be the one that goes down and heals him, but she will be the one that brings him back into the light where he belongs. As much as I would like nothing more than to deny that fact, I cannot. In planning all of this the way I did, I blocked out the part where I would not have been able to bring him into the light. It is specifically what Faith and others like her were made for and as such, they have to be the ones to see it through to the end.

It does not help that both Gabriel and her are smug now that they have laid their position out before me. I am sure it is not their intent to appear that way, but it is happening none the less. It is as if this is all a game to them. There is nothing about this undertaking that is a game and I want them to cease treating it as such immediately.

She has informed me of all she knows and despite my earlier assumptions about her, it does appear as if she has exhausted every avenue available in order to save his life. Watching the boy as I have been for the past few hours, in an effort to pick up on anything that might help us moving forward, he appears to be a lost cause. I just cannot say as much to Faith, because like my brother, she cares deeply for the human she is tasked with guarding over.

I will not deal with the boy in the manner she chooses to though. I have always hated that particular way of handling things. Gabriel does it the most, but Raphael and Uriel have also been known to do it on occasion. Entering into a human's sub conscious mind, speaking to them, it is offensive to my sensibilities. If we are to deal with them at all, we should stand before them in our true form and not hidden away the way they choose to.

We are angels. The highest order of the light known to mankind. We have no reason at all to hide. We see and know all and the humans would be better served seeing our strength, our level of power firsthand instead of having it come to them in healthy little doses.

"Your annoyance at the way things have to happen is well documented, brother. You do not need to focus so deeply on it. Doing so will only make the rest of Heaven pick up on it and that will spell disaster."

"Gabriel, all of Heaven is already aware of my feelings as it pertains to this matter. I will not hide it. You cannot tell me not to think or you open yourself up for me to do the same to you at a later date when you least expect it."

"You would relish that would you not?"

"It appears as though you know me better than I know myself. Remind me again why having her with me, other than to bring the boy back where he belongs, is the right move?"

"Despite your feelings regarding Faith, this situation with Colin, it is her Samael."

"Must you bring that up?"

"It is the only way I can think of to make you see it the way that I do. Just as you had been tasked with handling that particular situation, Faith is finding herself in the same place with the human."

"We are nothing alike."

"Precisely."

"Are you going to tell me what you mean by that or continue to be evasive?"

"Michael, what is it that Father tells us quite frequently that annoys us to no end? I cannot tell you that which you already know."

Gabriel quoting our father is a joke. It is made even worse that he is repeating our father's word back to me. It is usually the other way around. I do it with all of my brothers. Spending so much time with the Almighty the way I have, it seems right that the words of wisdom come from me when it cannot come from him. I am just not sure how I feel about the baby of the family being the one to do it now.

"You have never liked being told anything. You're the stubborn teenager."

"If that is how you see me than you must be the baby girl."

"Whenever emotion or feeling comes in conversation, you enjoy calling me a female. One of these days Michael, you will realize that the way I am has nothing to do with being female or male, but just in being."

"When did you become so wise?"

"While you had your head up Father's proverbial butt as they say."

I do believe the word he is looking for in this case is brownnoser, but I am not about to tell him that. I will never hear the end of it and as it stands, I have far too much to think about and plan now that I find myself saddled with a companion for my trip to the planet.

"Why does the prospect of traveling to Earth with Faith eat away at you in this way? It is like any other mission we have done together. The only difference in this case is that it is a female angel accompanying you."

I love Gabriel, of that there can be no doubt, but the way he is right now leaves something to be desired. I have seen the way him and the angel interact with each other. If that alone didn't irritate me to no end, knowing that I am travelling to the planet with her and they will be apart from one another is more than enough to do it.

"I prefer doing things on my own. It is less messy. I can be in and out with no real time spent away. In this regard, despite what you believe, I do not have that option and that is why this entire thing bothers me so deeply."

"Are you sure that is all it is?"

"What else could it be, Gabriel?"

He has been quick to answer the entire time he has been with me, yet that is not the case now. If I did not know any better it would appear as though he knows something that I am not aware of and is doing all he can to keep it from me.

"It is nothing, Michael. Father is due home any minute. I am sure that the two of you have much to discuss. As per our arrangement, I will not go to him until after you have both taken your leave, but you must prepare yourself for what will happen when you return. He will not be pleased knowing that a bringer of light is heading down to the planet."

Gabriel's words bring to the surface another concern of mine that I have given more than enough thought to over the last little while. Bringers of light are not permitted to leave Heaven. In taking Faith with me, I am going to earn Father's wrath the minute I return. I may be able to handle myself accordingly, but I did not look forward to what might happen to the ball of heavenly energy once the two of them came face to face. He would be far more lenient with me than with her, of that I was certain.

"I am well aware of how Father will feel about this when he finds out. Instead of standing here with me, expressing your thoughts on the matter, I do believe you should be saying all of this to her."

"It appears as though she knows what she is about to step into and will not listen to any more from me regarding it."

"Hmm, I do believe I like her after all."

"She was right earlier you know. You are a jerk."

"Sticks and stones, Gabriel."

I have to get him away from this topic of conversation. I cannot admit to him that I am going to handle this matter with Father when I return for the both of us because it will only give Gabriel the ammunition he needs to pester me further regarding her. Not to mention that despite my claims to the contrary every chance I get, I cannot seem to get the bringer of light out of my head.

The way she enters my thoughts and frustrates me so is off putting. I am unsure of what it is that is going on between us or even the first clue what to do with what is taking place. I have been around female angels before, there are a lot of them here, but never before have I experienced a reaction so strong with one.

It is another reason I am not looking forward to this trip. While I am here in Heaven, we have Gabriel as a go between, but the minute we head down to help Colin, he will be removed and it will just be the two of us. If earlier is any indication, the trip will not be an easy or pleasant one.

"Do you believe you can change this boy's path?"

He is unaware of it, but I am most thankful for his interruption and the subject change. With my thoughts deviating away from the task at hand and focusing on the most stubborn and obnoxious angel, any reprieve is welcome.

"I am going to make every feasible attempt at it. Lucifer has been reaching out to the humans lately in such a way that I fear we may never be able to save them all. I want to change the course with Colin. He will remain with us if I have anything to say about it."

"And if you fail in your attempt to save him?"

"There is no fail. I will do this, Gabriel. We will do this. Colin McDougall belongs in the light and I am going to make sure that I get him there. No matter what the cost."

Faith

This is really happening.

A vessel has been chosen and I am about to make my way from Heaven for the first time in my existence. Even though I am aware of the reason behind it, there is an excitement coursing through me at the mere thought of being a part of something Father put so much time into building that cannot be ignored.

With the way it has been treated in recent years, what our father intended so very long ago has been forgotten. In creating the world in the manner at which he did, it was his greatest accomplishment, the humans coming in right behind it. It is not often spoken about while I am in attendance, but after the events in the garden, Father saw fit to give the humans a level of free will previously unknown. He did not want to take their choice away and in doing so created something far more beautiful than anyone above or below can truly comprehend.

Most believe that free will is what turned the world so dark and allowed Lucifer the ability to reach out where he might not have been able to before, but I do not see it that way. I believe that even if everyone had acted the same, almost robotic in their movements and actions, he still would have gotten to them if he wanted to. Maybe that makes me naïve or just proves Michael's earlier assessment of what I am good for, but it is the way I am. I believe in giving the humans the option, he made his position and his belief in it known and we are only stronger because of it.

Sure, there are some that turn away from the light and no matter what is done to prevent it, we lose them, but it is those losses that have us coming back stronger and more determined than ever. The light will always win, no matter how many casualties we have along the way.

There is only one problem with what I believe and what I am about to do. I am going against Father in order to do it. Bringers of light like me, we are meant to operate from Heaven only. It is here that we are at our most powerful and it is here we are meant to always remain. In taking the step that I am now, I am breaking the rules. I am going against Father, following along with his most trusted son, in order to make things right for one human. If you look at it as some might, it would appear as though I am endangering the lives of millions to save the life of one, but I do not see it that way.

I do not want to go against Father and his original plan for me. I know that in doing so, I will be punished upon my return, but I cannot let it stop me. Father himself told me that Colin was meant for the light and I do not want to give up until I absolutely have to. Michael stepping forward and wanting to help, even if it did come at Gabriel's insistence, is my final shot at getting this right. I want to see this through, come home and show Father that despite breaking the rules, I have done the right thing.

I will settle for nothing less.

Taking this step, one would expect things to feel different, but everything seems to remain as it was. Angels flitter from one spot to another, each assigned their own tasks and focused on getting them done. They pay no attention to the angel standing just on the outskirts, awaiting word from an archangel that it is indeed time to make our way down. I am thankful for that. With as risky a move as this is, I want to be sure that it all goes off without a hitch.

Gabriel is staying behind in order to speak with Father about what Michael and I are about to face. He is going to stand, knowing what will come of it and speak up on our behalf because he believes just as I do that this is the last resort. The only bad part about him staying behind is that with as contemptuous as our relationship already is, there will be no one there to break us apart if things break down between his brother and me.

I know it was not his original plan and that the only reason I am even coming along for this is because he could not come up with an argument to fight me. I can only hope that as we make our way down and immerse ourselves in the human way of life that he does not hold that against me. If we are to save Colin in the way that I want, we are going to have to stay on the same page throughout the entire visit. I would like to say that it will be easy for me to do that, if I stay focused, but the truth is, with the way Michael makes me feel whenever we share the same space, I have a fear I will slip.

"Michael has chosen his vessel. It will only be a matter of time now before the two of you make your way down."

"Do you believe this is the right thing, Gabriel? Appearing to Colin in this way, is it really the only thing we have left to do?"

"You know as well as I do that everything else we have tried has not worked. I do not see any other alternative. Even though Michael wanted to move forward with this on his own, I do believe it is the right move."

"And Father?"

"I will handle our father, Faith. You must not concern yourself with that. All that you need to focus on is getting there and bringing the boy back to us the way you have been made to do. Michael and I can handle the rest."

"Why are you doing this for me?"

"Truthfully, at first I had no idea. I thought it was because of the way I felt when I with you. I have come to realize now, as more time has passed that it is more than that."

How he feels when he is with me?

"Surely by now you have noticed the connection we seem to have. It is most confusing of course, but welcome."

"You said that you realized now that it is more than that. What do you mean?"

"We are a great deal alike. We feel far too much for our own good, we want to do right by everyone we come into contact with and we will continue to take steps in order to do all of that even if the steps are not the ones that are right."

"So you are helping me because we are alike?"

"In a manner of speaking yes." He answers with a curt nod. "None of this matters though. What does matter is, are you sure you are ready for everything you are about to witness the minute you leave here?"

There is a moment after he nods that I sense there is more he wants to say, but with the change in attitude that occurs almost immediately afterward, it is almost as if I imagined the entire thing.

"I have no other choice but be ready, Gabriel. I have heard a great deal about the way Michael operates when on missions for our father. He deserves nothing less than the best."

"He is getting the best in you. He is just unaware of it."

"What do you mean by that?"

"Michael, despite appearing otherwise, was deeply hurt by what occurred on his last mission. He is not the same brother that left here months ago. He returned different and I do believe that in doing this with you, it will bring the old Michael back to us."

"What was the mission?"

"He had to assassinate one of our brothers. It was not a pretty experience and is one of the downfalls of what we do here. I cannot say more as it is not my story to tell, but as I said before, it is my hope that travelling with you, the angel that you are, will help bring him back."

"You think I can save him?"

"Not save per say. He is not entirely lost to us. There are parts of him that are buried under the tough exterior he puts forth, but he is still very much alive underneath it all. I can see it every time I speak with him. You, every step you take is guided by the light, an innate goodness deep inside. You feel and experience all that comes along with feeling and I do believe that right now, that is exactly what Michael needs."

"I somehow doubt he would agree with that."

He laughs and the tension I had not even realized built inside me melted away at the sound. The range of emotions and experiences I am already going through and we haven't even left yet is almost too much to take. I had been excited at the prospect of doing this, saving someone in this way, then worried about Father's reaction and now I'm weighed down by the daunting task that Gabriel has inadvertently placed before me.

"There is not much that I say that Michael would agree with. I am sure you have seen that already. He is not the most personable angel."

"Understatement of the century."

"Faith, despite the way Michael has appeared to be with you, there is more to him. I want you to remember that most of all as you make this journey to Earth."

"Is there any other advice you want to give before he calls for me?"

"No. I do believe that you will handle what needs to be done in a manner that will make all beings of the light proud. I do have a request though."

"What would that be?

"When you have saved Colin, as I know that both you and Michael will do, bring my brother home to me."

"Well I did not plan on leaving him on the planet, Gabriel." I say, laughing, but not feeling it all the way through. I can sense that he means more, but focusing on it will only make me nervous again and that is something that right now I cannot afford.

"That is not what I meant."

"Then what do you mean?"

"You have within you the ability to heal the parts of Michael that are most displaced. Faith, you are the only one capable of doing it. So when everything is said and done, bring my brother home to me, the one he is meant to be."

Chapter Eight

Michael

I knew with everything I had seen before coming down here that where we found Colin would not be pretty, but the scene I am witnessing before me now, turns my stomach as it reminds me of times past.

Not long ago, I had found Samael in a place very similar to this. Knowing he had been caught in his double dealing with both Heaven and Hell, he had taken to another realm and in doing so, found himself in a place as cold and dank as the one Colin finds himself now.

It is not supposed to concern me how the bringer of light is handling this, but I cannot help taking her in as she witnesses the scene before her. When we watch from home, it never appears quite as real as it does in the moment and seeing her face scrunch up at not only the smell, but what she is witnessing in terms of the location and the way the boy looks, I am troubled.

She needs to come to terms with how dark things have truly gotten with the boy before we can move forward with what needs to be done. If she goes into this with rose colored glasses, not seeing everything for what it is, it will spell disaster and we will lose the boy forever.

I remember vividly the first time I came here. Father insisted that in order for us to grow and become what he had made all of us to be, we had to see things firsthand. It was not nearly as dark as this particular scene, but it had been an eye opening experience for me and I can tell as she takes it all in, it is much the same for her. This moment, right now, will change everything for her, forever. Faith will not go home the same.

None of us ever do.

"Faith, are you alright?"

"Yeah—I'm fine." She answers, the crack in her voice more noticeable than I am sure she intended. "Can I ask you something?"

"Of course."

"The way it all appears, why are we not shown that from home?"

"It is shown that way. There are just some beings that Father has chosen to hide the reality from."

"So before you came here, you saw the truth? You knew it was this bad?"

Her tone lowers and I can tell that my answer has caused her pain. While I am sure she knew that all of Heaven was not equal, it is obvious she hoped it was possible.

"Yes. For you, given what it is that you do, there is a haze of sorts placed over the humans, so that you are protected from seeing how bad it can get. I never did agree much with Father choosing to do it that way, but it is what it is."

"You think I should know what I'm getting into?"

"Don't you?" I question, not wanting to focus on what it is I believe should happen in Heaven. I may have had power during Father's absence, but that did not mean I had it now that he was back. I have no right to question why Father does the things he does.

"I would have thought that was obvious."

"It does not matter what I believe, Faith."

I want to say more of course. For some reason I cannot ascertain, I want to tell her why I believe differently because I do believe she will understand, but I cannot do it. We are here to focus on a specific task and I cannot take away from that. The sooner we do what we came here to do, the sooner we can get back home and things can go back to normal again.

We can go back and I can be rid of this angel and the irritating sensations she evokes inside me, never to come across her again.

"One's beliefs always matter, Michael."

Of course she has to say something like that. I should have seen this type of answer coming, but with her I can never be sure of anything. The intense loathing I felt at home with her, is now replaced with something else and it disturbs me to no end. No being should be this hard to figure out. Faith is an enigma.

"Tell me what you are experiencing right now." I demand, ignoring her response and choosing instead to get back to the task at hand.

"A few days ago, he appeared to be close to the edge. What I see now, everything placed the way it is, where he finds himself, even the way he looks, it is far worse than I imagined."

"Now you see why Gabriel brought this to me. The real truth."

She nods her head, her hand coming up to rest over her lips. She is deeply affected by the scene before her and despite my claim not to care, not wanting to be anywhere near any instance of real feeling, especially where this angel is concerned, I find myself wanting to reach out to her. I want to lessen the blow of this experience for her.

I do not want what she is witnessing to change her so completely the way I know it will.

"Are we too late?"

"Why would you ask something like that?"

"There are track marks on his arms. I am aware of them as he has had them almost as long as I have been watching over him, but there are almost double the normal amount now. He no longer lives in the apartment he resided in days ago and finds himself here, in the middle of nowhere, no other living human around him, cold and alone. The shivering he is experiencing in his sleep this way, are the nightmares breaking through again. I am used to it, but not to this degree. Michael, are we too late?"

"No, Faith we are not." I am aware of how deeply the boy has fallen just in our time apart from him, but I am confident in my belief that we are not too late. "I know the way he appears to you and how hard all of this must be to witness, it being your first time here and all, but we still have time to break through. We can save him."

Her eyes, which had been leveled directly on the boy in front of her now lift until I can feel them trained on me. She may not be looking me in the eye, but the intense heat from her stare alone is enough to set my very human vessel ablaze.

I tried to ignore it, when she chose her vessel and stepped into it for the first time, but the longer we stand here alone, the harder it is to block out. She had been glorious bathed in only the light of home, but now, in her vessel, she is breathtaking.

Her dark brown hair cascades down around her shoulders, her brown eyes are smoldering, almost as if there are secrets buried deep inside them that no one else is privileged enough to know. She stands close to my tall frame, where at home she had been significantly smaller. I should not be focusing on the way she appears, and more on getting her through this so that we can help the boy under her charge, but the more time that passes, the harder is becomes to look away.

It is as if I need to acknowledge her for some reason I do not understand.

"You really believe that, don't you?"

"If I look at it any other way, I would be going against all that I have been taught and shown. Of course I believe in what we are here to accomplish. Are you telling me you do not?"

"I don't know what to believe in anymore."

"Do not let what you have learned here change what you believe to be the truth. If you feel that it is happening, please do the one thing that until now you have found most difficult to do."

"What would that be?"

"Believe in me."

Chapter Nine

Faith

If the scene I witnessed the moment we came across Colin for the first time was not painful enough, what happened next surely is.

I am beginning to see now why Father chooses to keep us so close to home, not letting us experience this firsthand. It is because what the humans in our charge go through, what brings them to us to begin with, is too much to bear. It may have offended me, finding out from Michael that the way things are shown to me is not the way it appears for others, but the more time I spend watching Colin, I am beginning to see the reasoning behind it.

Since arriving, my unwilling partner in this mission has changed from the way he appeared at home. Where he had been brash and cold before, he now appears almost sympathetic to what I am going through. His final words to me before I asked him to remove himself from the room speak to it.

"Believe in me."

Believing in the archangel that had done nothing but get under my skin from the moment I met him is the very last thing I want to do, but with everything I have learned, it is something I feel I may have to do in order to make it through what we must do now.

As we stood watching the boy, he began to shift in his place on the filth covered mattress he finds himself on and it was then that I asked Michael to take his leave. Knowing that he has to be here; that he will be the one to help me bring this boy back into the light had not slipped my mind, I just felt that it would easier for Colin to see me alone. With the strain he is already under, seeing two angels standing before him may not go over well and right now, if we want this to succeed, every step has to be taken with a level of care previously unknown.

As it turns out, asking the angel to leave had not been the right decision after all. What I assumed would be easy, turned out to be so much more.

*****

"What—who are you? What are you doing here? How did you get in? What do you want?"

For someone who only a few seconds before had been at rest, no matter how uncomfortable it might have been, the amount of questions that flood the room is startling.

"Colin, please do not be afraid."

"Easy for you to say. Who the hell are you and what the hell do you think you're doing standing over me like that?"

"We have spoken before, on more than one occasion. My name is Faith."

"This is some sort of sick joke right? Who are you really? Did Marcus send you?"

I am aware of who Marcus is. It is the human that Colin gets the narcotics from and someone I want nothing more than to deal with personally when my time here is done. He is feeding these drugs so easily into bodies he has no right to. He needs to be stopped, of that I am sure.

"Marcus did not send me and I assure you, there is nothing funny about this situation."

"So, the voice in my head, the one that keeps telling me that I need to keep fighting, that's you?"

I nod and he frowns. He does not believe what I am telling him, but that was expected. I am standing here now, much the same way as he is, in a human vessel. I can only imagine that the jump between a voice in the mind to a physical body is a hard leap to take.

In admitting to him who I am, I thought it would bring him a level of calm. He no longer had to feel as though he was crazy, that I am indeed real the way I told him, but the look in his eyes at my nod is anything but comforting and calm.

Within seconds he leaps from his place on the bed and his arms are gripping mine tightly, a look in his eyes so cold it sends a shiver down my very human spine. Removing one of his hands from around my arm he brings it up to my neck and the shiver I experienced only seconds before turns into a full on shake.

"You're lying! Marcus sent you. He wants his money, but he's not getting it until I get what I paid for! You hear me bitch? Give me the stuff!"

There is no way with the hold he has on my neck now that I can answer him, so using the full force of the body I find myself in, I begin to thrash about, hoping that in doing so I can take him off guard and he will loosen his grip, giving me the escape I so desperately need.

When I've successfully broken away from him, my hand instantly going to my throat as I attempt to suck in as much air as possible, a breeze floats in around me and I realize I am no longer alone. Before I can call out and stop him, I watch as Michael makes his way around me and straight for the damaged boy standing angrily above me.

"Give me one reason why I should not kill you where you stand!" he yells at Colin, his voice as cold as ice. Watching as he grabs him by the throat, I realize that I am seeing Michael in his true way of being now. This is not the angel that spoke to me earlier, but the warrior.

The protector.

"Who the fuck are you?" Colin chokes out, his eyes level with Michael's chest, the anger clearly evident, yet not quite as potent as minutes before.

"Your worst nightmare."

"Michael, release the boy. He is not responsible for his actions."

With as determined as he is, I do not expect him to do as I have asked, but after a few seconds, he releases the hold around Colin's neck and the boy falls, sliding down onto the floor, as if defeated.

"From this moment forward, I am not leaving you alone with him again. Do I make myself clear?"

Not trusting my voice to speak, the fear from the altercation with Colin still fresh, I merely nod and lower my gaze to the floor.

"You are right. He is not in his right mind, but if I had not walked in when I did, there is no telling what the boy would have done to you. You do not have the power level that you normally do when at home. There would be nothing that you could have done had he taken it any further."

He does not need to explain this to me. I am more than aware of what could have happened. For whatever reason, coming to Colin this way had not worked out at all the way I wished for it too and now we were all paying the price.

"I thought that appearing to him alone would go easier than if he woke up and saw the two of us standing over him. Surely you can see my logic in doing it that way."

"I have no idea what you are talking about."

"I may not know all there is to know about humans, Michael, but when a guy of your size stands over someone when they first wake up, I have to assume there is going to be a moment of resistance. A reaction. I did not want to cause the boy any more pain than he is already experiencing."

"So leaving yourself open for an attack is the proper way to go is it?"

Whatever I may have felt from him earlier, when we stood together watching over our charge is gone now. Michael may have acted like he cared before, but it is clear now that is all it was. An act. He is still the same cold, unfeeling bastard he was before we made our way down here.

"This cold, unfeeling bastard just saved your life. I do believe a bit of gratitude is customary in instances such as this."

"That won't ever happen," I answer easily. *"I would not want to inflate your already oversized ego."*

*****

There can be no denial that in arriving when he did, he stopped what could have been a disastrous situation, but there is no way I was going to thank him for it. I went into the situation believing that Colin would easily come to terms with me standing before him and had been wrong. It was a mistake, but not something I needed to be berated over.

So here we stand, Michael on one side of the room and me on the other, Colin between us, watching as he attempts to come to terms with what is taking place around him.

Once he recovered from Michael grabbing him, he scurried back quickly onto his bed and had not looked in our direction once. Coming here, there had been a set plan on how we wanted to handle this situation, but the more time spent here, Colin reacting the way he is, that plan is quickly being thrown out the window.

It appears as though, with as hard as he was to break through to in Heaven, he will also be here and not only am I learning it, but Michael is as well.

"Who are you really?" Colin asks, finally speaking up. "If Marcus didn't send you than who did?"

"No one sent us, human. We are here because it is painfully obvious you are in need of an intervention."

"Michael, do you have to be harsh with him?"

"Do you have to be so attentive? We are here to save the boy or have you forgotten that? The time for being attentive is over."

"A little compassion won't kill you."

Where I expect there to be some response, there is none. It would appear as though, again, just as I did at home before our departure, I have made the archangel quiet. Seizing the opportunity, I turn toward Colin again. It is time for me to run things my way since Michael's way seems to be getting us nowhere.

"As I tried to explain to you when you woke, my name is Faith. I am the person you've been speaking to for the past several months."

His eyes lift at the soothing sound of my voice and it takes everything in me not to turn and smile at Michael in satisfaction. I may not have gone about things the right way at first, but it is obvious my second attempt is the one that will work.

"How are you talking in my head like that? You some kind of witch or something?"

Do not even think of it, Faith. You are not to tell him what you are.

I may have been stripped of my light before joining with the vessel, but it appears as though Michael did not experience the same thing as his voice booms loud and clear inside my head, unwanted and as per his usual, annoying.

"No. I assure you, I am not a witch. I am merely someone that cares a great deal about you and can no longer watch as you fill your body with the substances that threaten to kill you."

"Don't you get it lady? I'm ready to die. There's nothing to live for."

Michael takes a step forward and I come out in front of him, blocking him from whatever it is he is attempting to do. There is no way I am letting the angel near Colin now that I have him opening up. Whatever Michael wants to do is going to have to wait. We are playing this my way.

"If the boy wants to die that badly, I can oblige him."

"That is not what we are here to do, or did you forget that already?"

Again, he falls silent at my words and this time, I do not hold back. I smile. It would seem that even with as annoyed as he is with me, he is still willing to back down over the truth I am leveling him with.

"What the hell are you two talking about?" Colin interrupts and taking a chance, I turn from Michael and make my way over to bed, sitting ever so gently on the end of the mattress and turning my body toward his.

"We are here to help you, Colin. I know that with everything that has happened recently, it appears otherwise, but I assure you, all we want to do is help. You are not meant to die."

"How you gonna help me?"

"Getting that junk out of your bloodstream would be a start." Michael snaps, causing me to turn again and level him with a death glare. Why couldn't Gabriel be the one to come down with me? Surely I wouldn't have this much trouble with the other archangel. Where he seemed to get it, Michael does not.

"Michael, I think it best if you leave. You are not helping the situation."

"I am not going anywhere."

"Colin was not in his right mind earlier. He is now. I will be safe."

"I do not care if you believe yourself to be safe or not. I am not going anywhere. Do whatever you wish with the boy, but I will not leave you alone with him."

"Can you just stop this bullshit and tell me what the hell is going on? My head's starting to hurt keeping up with you two."

I know what I have to do now. Nothing but the truth is going to work with Colin and quite frankly, with the experiences he has already gone through in his life, the pain and agony he feels, he deserves that and so much more. If we are to do what we have been sent down here to do, it has to be this way.

I have got to tell him the truth, about everything, no matter what punishment I face from Michael and even Father when I finally make my way home.

"Colin, I know the way that we appear to you, but there is something you must know."

"Faith, do not do this—" Michael interjects, attempting to stop me from what I know now is the only way we can move forward and end this man's struggle once and for all.

"I am able to contact you through your mind because I'm not human."

Knowing Michael is not pleased, but too afraid to look at him in order to see his reaction firsthand, I forge ahead. Turning my attention back to Colin, I level him with the brightest smile I can bring to the surface and when he does not look away, I do what I believe to be the right thing.

I tell him everything.

"I am an angel of Heaven and I have been sent here to bring you back into the light, where you belong."

Chapter Ten

Michael

This should have been a routine assignment for me, but it is quickly turning into anything but and there is only one reason for it. The bringer of light.

There was a reason I wanted to come to the planet and handle this myself. I could have easily appeared before the boy in my true form, garnered what I needed from him in order to join together as one, healed him and been on my way. As it stands now, none of that is happening and I am at a loss as to what to do to change it.

I do not work well with other angels. That is not to say that I do not go on missions with my brothers and appreciate what each of them bring to the table when we are in combat together, but lesser angels, ones that are not aware of the true evil we are facing, I do not work with them. They are nothing but a hindrance to me, as Faith is now proving with her over the top antics.

The reason for choosing vessels and making our way down the way we did is so that we could grow closer to the boy without plunging him further into the darkness that's present in him. We have not been here long and already she is blowing that completely, choosing to go about things in her own way. A way that will end up costing us when we do get to go home again.

I need to put a stop to this, but I am finding myself unable to do so. For whatever reason, the softness in her eyes, the almost lyrical sound of her voice, it is having the desired effect on the boy. He is entranced by her, unable to look away. Only able to listen as she speaks the truth to him. It is because of this I cannot stop her.

"You're an angel?"

"Yes."

"You have any idea how crazy that sounds lady? Angels aren't real."

"I know it appears that way, but you could not be further from the truth, Colin. We are very real. I am living proof."

"Let's say I believe you, why do the angels suddenly give a damn about me now?"

"We have always cared about you."

"That's bullshit."

His level of disbelief in her words seems to surprise her, but it has the opposite effect on me. The majority of humans are this way. They have been so conditioned to believe that just because we do not appear to them in the darkest moments and answer their prayers right when they are sent, we do not exist. Even now, standing before him the way we are, he cannot believe because in his mind, if we were real we would have prevented everything he has gone through.

The reality of the situation is, everything he experienced he had to go through in order to be prepared for his future within the light. Where all beings of light have a purpose, so do the humans. They experience the majority of the dark times because they are learning. Not everything they go through is meant to happen, especially as it pertains to the darkness, but there can be no denial that even the darkest moment in a person's life can be a learning experience.

"Let me start from the beginning. That may help you come to terms with everything more quickly."

There she goes again. Attempting to reach out to the boy by giving him all the facts even though she is breaking every conceivable rule in order to do so. I need to put an end to this before she takes it too far, but just as I was before, I am frozen in place.

"I am what Heaven refers to as a bringer of light. I am tasked with guarding over humans like you that seem to be walking a fine line between good and evil. It is my job to bring you back into the light where you belong."

"You ever have someone you can't save?"

She lowers her head and speaks, this time, the sound of her voice coming out significantly lower than times before.

"Yes. There have been a few over the years that I have not been able to save. Ones I have lost to the darkness. It is those losses that push me this time. I do not want to lose you Colin. I want to bring you back into the light."

"And if that's not possible? If I'm too far gone to be saved?"

"I cannot answer that because I do not believe you to be that lost."

If I was not witnessing this with my own eyes I would not believe it. The human whose body before had been frigid and cold, unwilling to hear anything she had to say, no matter how filled with truth it was, is now turned toward her, his body language signaling that he is indeed open to hearing more, learning as it were. It appears as though her attempt is working much better than I believed it ever would.

Despite being unable to feel much of anything since my battle with Samael, I cannot deny that in this instance, I am feeling things, one particular thing stronger than all others.

I am impressed.

Faith

The entire time I have been sitting here, explaining things to Colin, Michael has been silent. I should not be concerning myself with it, but I am unable to think of much else.

I want to turn around and face the angel that is here with me now. I want to know how he feels about what I am doing, but I cannot. I do not want to admit it, but seeing disappointment in his eyes will remind me of all I am doing wrong and with the way Colin seems to be responding to everything I am saying, the last thing I want is to feel as though any of this is wrong.

"If you want to save me so badly, if you believe that I'm destined for the light or whatever, where the hell were you when I needed you most?"

Before I even open my mouth to give him the answers he seeks, Michael clears his throat from behind me and despite not wanting to turn around, I have no other choice but do just that because not only does he clear his throat but he speaks.

"I do believe this is where my expertise comes into play."

"I know what she is, but what are you?"

"If you think about it, I am sure it will come to you rather easily."

"Probably could do that, but why don't you just tell me instead?" Colin asks, this time his lips raising just slightly until he is smirking at the angel standing stiff as ever in the corner of the room.

"Michael is an archangel." I answer before Michael has the chance to. I can only imagine how much he hates being here as I break every rule imaginable, so the least I can do is soften the blow.

"The bringer of light speaks the truth. I am an archangel. It is of little importance to me what the two of you are speaking about. The reason she did not appear to you when as you say, you needed her most is because at that point she had not even been made aware of you."

Colin turns back to me, the smirk from only a few seconds before gone and his face now a mask of seriousness again.

"Is that true?"

"Yes. I learned of you at your creation but I was not permitted to get involved."

"Why is that? Aren't you guys supposed to be about doing right by people?"

I want to answer this, but I am worried that my answer will not be the one he wants to hear, which will in the end only make him pull away again, something I cannot afford now that I have been able to break through his well-constructed walls.

"It is not that cut and dry."

Turning at the sound of Michael speaking again, I lock eyes with him and the hardness I witnessed only minutes before is gone, replaced by something else entirely. If I did not know any better I would think he heard my thoughts and was doing what is needed in order to make things easier for me.

Michael making anything easier for me is preposterous. Despite the way he appears now, he has made his position clear from the beginning and I need to remember that even though the soft blue of his eyes is most difficult to tear myself away from.

"Well, I've got nothing but time, man. Why don't you explain it to me?"

"You do not have that much time, I assure you. Explaining the way Heaven operates, would take longer than a normal human lifetime. Yours being as close to its end as it is, I would definitely not finish my explanation in time."

Colin seems to take in what Michael is saying as I watch his head dip toward the cement floor below us. Michael may have told him in a way that I would not, but there can be no denial of the truth. He is indeed close to his end, which is why we are appearing before him this way and as much as I want to hide that from him, I know he has every right to know. It could be the very thing that saves his life.

"Am I really that close to dying?"

"Dying is the least of your concerns human."

"Oh really? What's worse than dying?"

"I would think the fires of hell would concern you more than an insignificant human death."

"Excuse me?"

Not sure if it will work the same way as it did with him earlier, but knowing that right now I needed to put an end to the turn this conversation is taking, I reach out to Michael and pray as I do that it works and I can stop him before he reaches a point of no return. When I broke the rules in order to tell Colin the truth, I accepted it, but I cannot accept Michael doing the same.

If you can hear me, please stop. This is too much information for him to process. I do believe it is time we got back to what we have been sent here to do.

After a few minutes pass, watching for any sign that Michael had heard my plea, I give up. It is obvious that while Michael retained all of his power because of his position in Heaven, I have not.

You have more power than you think, Faith. I will refrain from giving the boy any more information, but you owe me.

Pleased that he had heard my plea and would not proceed any further, ignoring the rest of what he said, not wanting to acknowledge owing him anything, I turn my attention back to Colin and pick up where Michael left off.

"You must excuse Michael, he does not interact with humans very often."

How very human of you, Faith. Exploiting my weaknesses is not your smartest move.

Ignoring his voice as best I can, I focus again on Colin and what we are here to do. Michael can believe I am picking on him all he wants, but from where I sit, I am only stating the obvious.

"What did he mean by the fires of hell?"

"You are meant for the light as I have said, but there is also something far more sinister in nature that wants you as well. It is that which brings us here now."

"Yeah, great. We're back to the whole you saving me thing again."

"I am aware of everything you have been through and I am also aware of how badly you want the pain to cease, but ending your life is not the right way to handle things."

"Then what do you suggest I do?"

"Let us do what we have been sent to do." I answer easily, not giving my answer a second thought.

"What exactly does that mean? What do you want to do with me?"

Michael again chooses that moment to speak, cutting me off before I can say what it is that needs to be done.

"Possess you."

Chapter Eleven

Michael

It had not been an easy sell, getting the boy to understand what it is we must do in order to set things right again. There had been moments at which I believed that he would be lost to us forever, but as I have come to notice in my short time working with the bringer of light, she does not give up easily.

When the human appeared to be distancing himself from our explanations, believing them to be false, all it would take is one look from her, or the smallest touch to his bare skin and he was right back on board again. I am not sure if it is part of the way she was made, but the human is powerless against her. He will bend to her willingly because he is captivated by her.

Just as I am.

Never in all the time that has passed since my creation have I had a reaction to another being this way. It has gotten so bad that any attempt I make at blocking the way she affects me fails at every turn because it pains me to turn away from her. She is speaking to the human in the most beautiful tone of voice, reminiscent of the music that only beings of the light can make and there can be no doubt that in doing so, she has wrapped both me and the human up in a spell that we are powerless to break free of.

There is not much that I am afraid of, but the way at which this angel gets to me, both on a human and celestial level is enough to bring fear alive in me. I have no experience with the way she seems to call to me. I have moved closer to her in the last few minutes and have been completely unaware that it is even happening. I am drawn to her for some reason I cannot ascertain and it is making me uncomfortable.

I need to get a handle on this and I need to do it soon. I am about to join with the human now that he has given us his consent and I need to put my entire focus into that, healing the boy from the inside out in order to make things right again.

In order to make things right for Faith.

"Michael, is everything okay?"

"Yes, of course it is. Why do you ask?"

"We have been ready for the last fifteen minutes, but have been waiting on you."

In an attempt to block out what is building inside of my human vessel because of my reaction to the bringer of light, I turned away from the conversation and with the way she is looking at me now, those deep brown eyes staring a hole straight into my own, I know that I have been caught. By the very being causing it all to begin with, no less.

"My apologies. I was giving you and the human a chance to connect. I was unaware that I had stepped away quite so much."

"You do not need to apologize, Michael. I was merely concerned about you."

What is this sensation I am experiencing? The one that makes me want to reach out to her and bring her close to me? I went into this undertaking with the knowledge that I would experience things as a human, it is inevitable, but this is a reaction I am most unfamiliar with. It is more than a want. I could handle a want. This is a need and it is something I most definitely cannot handle, even with the large amount of heavenly power at my disposal.

"Michael," she sighs, bringing my attention again back to her. "You lied to me."

"I have no idea what you mean. How do you figure I have lied?"

"There is something going on with you. I am unsure of what it might be, but there can be no denial of it. You are distant, even more so than before. We are mere seconds away from completing what we came here to do, but you seem to be anywhere but here."

"I assure you, I am right where I need to be. You have caught me thinking is all."

"Do you want to tell me what it is you are thinking about?"

"No particularly. It is none of your concern, angel."

"Well, in that case, shall we get on with the real reason we are here?"

"I would like nothing more."

As she turns from me, there is an ache in my chest like none other I have experienced before and I want nothing more in the moment than to turn her around again, so that she can face me as I bring her into me. Resisting the urge, burying it down as deeply as I can manage, I put my focus back where it belongs.

I have a human that I need to join with in an effort to make things right. Whatever this is, between the bringer of light and myself, it is going to have to wait. Nothing can get in the way of what I am about to do.

When I am finished with my reason for being here, I can handle Faith and whatever it is that she is doing to me.

I could put an end to this once and for all.

Faith

I have done my best answering all of Colin's questions, even going so far as to speak to him about what he could expect joining together with Michael even though I have no real experience with possession. This is where Michael would come in handy, but it appears as though he has something more pressing going on that is pulling him farther away from what is taking place here.

With what Gabriel spoke to me about before we left to come here, I thought it might have had something to do with that, but after reaching out to him in an effort to get him to open up about it and being shot down, I am at a loss to where I am supposed to go from here.

There is something troubling him, there is no doubt about that if the expressions on his face are any indication. They filter from one to the other so quickly, if it had been anyone else witnessing it I am sure they would not have caught them all, but with nothing to do but wait for him to come around, I am able to see and experience them all for myself.

Could he still be troubled from the mission he recently returned home from? Is it indeed what Gabriel said and he is separating himself from all of us and needs a push in order to come back around? Can I really be the one to bring him back to the way he used to be the way Gabriel seems to think?

"I know what she told me, but when this is over, how do you know it worked?"

"Well for us, we will be able to see a light around you. Faith has bared witness to your light for years, but as it appears to us now, it is dull and as lifeless as you yourself appear to be. When I am finished with you, it will be bright again and the heaviness that you feel on your heart will no longer exist."

"What does that mean exactly?" Colin asks, his confusion at Michael's words evident.

"It means that you will be able to breathe easier. The urge that you have inside of you for your next fix, it will no longer be there. You will feel alive for the first time in years." I answer, hoping that my explanation is easier to understand than that of the impersonal archangel now kneeling over the bed, preparing himself for what is about to happen next.

"You can take my addiction away?"

"Yes. We can take it all away, Colin. You were never meant for this path. It is time we rectify that."

"I know we've gotta do this, but I've got one more question."

"Ask whatever you wish. I will answer to the best of my ability."

"Why do you care so much?"

As the question falls, I not only feel his eyes on me but Michaels as well, which does nothing to help me in answering. I have been asked this question before, on numerous occasions so it should come easy for me, but for some reason, in this instance it feels different somehow. It is as if I am not answering Colin's question, but Michael's.

The easy answer is that it is my job to care. It is what I am supposed to do as an agent of Heaven and a being of light, but there is more to it for me. I have no idea if it works that way for the other bringers, but for me it has always been about more than just a task I am assigned to complete.

I care about the humans in my charge because I see myself in them. I am not without failing even though I am made from the purest light imaginable. I have doubts just as they do, I do things wrong, as is apparent in not being able to save the ones I have lost over the years. I am just like them and it is because of that, I care as deeply as I do. That is what I want everyone to know, but have spent so long not admitting to.

"I care because we are not so different. Just as God made you, he also made me."

"I'm pretty sure you've never been through anything like this." Colin whispers motioning around him as if where he finds himself is all the answer I need.

"But I have, don't you see? I am experiencing every bit of this with you."

The room falls silent after that and the more time that stretches with no movement or words spoken, the more uncomfortable I feel. Had I said too much? Would speaking the truth the way I felt it end up doing more damage?

Do not think that way. What you said was perfect.

Anytime Michael enters my mind this way, it almost feels like a violation, other than the one time that he answered in order to let me know he had heard me speak to him. I do not like the way it feels having him inside of me this way, even if what he says is comforting. He has not earned the right to hear my most intimate thoughts. That is reserved for me only.

If you do not wish me to be privy to what you are thinking, perhaps you can stop thinking so loudly.

"I'll remember that next time." I say, aloud this time in an attempt to make a point. I want him out of my head and I want him out now. We've got much more important things to be concerning ourselves with. My thoughts should not even register.

"Colin, are you ready for this? It will not be the most comfortable experience."

"I'm as ready as I'm ever gonna be." He says, but as Michael moves closer in an effort to begin joining, he speaks again. "Thank you for never giving up, Faith; even when I did."

Chapter Twelve

Faith

Colin McDougall looks as beautiful now as he did the day he was brought into the world. Where the light then had wrapped itself up so completely in his tiny, fragile frame, it is now doing the same as Michael and I watch in amazement. Well, I am watching that way. I am sure what Michael is experiencing is much different, but it is no less beautiful.

This is the way things were always meant to be. Colin was meant to have this light surrounding him, the smile now lifting his entire face should never have been taken from him. When he mentioned us being created to do right by people earlier, it is in this moment that the statement is most true. We had done right by him and no matter what I face leaving this place now, I know nothing will ever compare to it again.

With our task complete, we need to head back to Heaven, but I find myself unable to move from my spot to the right of the bed. Watching Colin as he sleeps peacefully for the first time in years, I want nothing more than to stay here with him forever. The darkness that had taken over his life, I want to protect him from. Michael may have healed him and taken all of the true evil away, but it would still be a tough road ahead for the human boy.

The first step being getting him out of this place he finds himself in. I am not sure I can leave until I know that there is somewhere safer than this.

"Do you ever stop caring about them, even when you have completed your assigned task?" The low voice breaks through, tearing me away from the picture before me and my thoughts and focusing me solely on him.

"No, but I am sure you already knew that."

"I did."

"Then why even ask the question?"

"For some reason I cannot ascertain, I enjoy it when you speak, even when it is filled with annoyance the way it is now."

"I am not annoyed with you."

"I did not say that you were, but thank you for proving my point."

There is something I have noticed about Michael since coming here and spending time with him this way. Even after doing what he did, saving Colin from Lucifer's clutches, he does not smile. I have done nothing but smile and show happiness and elation at what has taken place, but Michael remains the same as he has always been. It is upsetting to me but I do not dare bring it up to him. The icy demeanor of before has thankfully not made another appearance. If I bring up his inability to smile, it will surely bring it back in full force.

"May I ask you something?"

"After what we have experienced with the boy sleeping soundly before us, you may ask me anything you wish."

"The mission you were on before coming home and stepping in for our father, what happened?"

Asking a question like this, I thought I knew what to expect, but as I am quickly beginning to learn with this archangel, nothing will ever go as expected. His body, which had been completely at ease, taking in just as I am the picture of peace before us, is now rigid and no doubt cold. Whatever he had been through was a lot harder than Gabriel made it out to be.

"Why of all the things you can ask me, is that what you chose to start with?"

"Despite your best attempts at masking it, there is something that your mind cannot seem to let go of. It has taken you away from this place numerous times since we arrived and I have a feeling it is something pertaining to what you went through then."

"You make a lot of assumptions based on a few hours spent together."

"Maybe so, but I do not hear you denying it."

"What I experienced before Gabriel came to see me about your little problem, I am not sure I can speak about it, least of all with you."

"Why do you do that?"

"I am unsure what you mean."

"You can accuse me of making assumptions all you want, but whenever I seem to get too close to something, you turn it around and somehow find a way to attack me. I may not be an archangel like you, but that does not mean I am any less important."

He falls silent and I cannot help feeling proud that I am able to put him in his place. It is only when he raises his head and I see the pained expression on his face that the elation that I feel at having bested him fades away and is replaced with something I am most unfamiliar with.

I am experiencing his hurt as if it is my own.

"You do not need to tell me what happened to you. I am sorry for even bringing it up."

"No, you are right. I have been treating you as though you are less than me. I am wrong. You are not less, Faith. In fact, after what we have been through here today, I am beginning to see that you may just be more."

Well this was not the way I saw this conversation going when I started it. Michael admitting to me that he was wrong does not seem as right as it should. I can tell it is something he does not do often as it seems to cause him no small level of agony having to admit to it at all.

"There is no truth in that statement, Michael. You being the one to heal Colin in the way you did proves that you are important, more so than I am. What I was unable to accomplish, you did easily."

"You do not see it do you? The only reason that boy let me within two feet of him today, especially after the way I introduced myself into the situation, is because of you and the way you reached out to him."

"I have been doing that from Heaven for ages."

"Yes, you have, but for Colin, I do believe it was the honest approach you took with him, coupled with the vessel you took that was able to finally break through. What you could not do at home, you did here with ease. I may have been the one to heal him, but you are the one that saved him."

This is where we will never see eye to eye. I do believe that in some way, our levels of importance are the same, but there can be no doubt that Michael is the stronger one. He had been the one to reach inside of the boy and put back together what had been so tragically ripped apart. We may be equally important, but we would never truly be equals.

Michael is everything that I cannot be.

"You fight against me when I make light of you and your abilities, yet freely do the same to yourself. Why is that?"

For the first time since speaking with him, I have no easy answer. He is right. When he attacks me for being a bringer of light, or less than him, I go on the defense immediately, but when the same happens at my own hand, I am noticeably silent. There is no explanation I can give that will make sense.

"Before Gabriel came to me," Michaels says, this time noticeably quieter than before. "I had just gotten back from a situation that even now, disturbs me to no end, but not because of what I had to do. I have come to terms with that easily. It is everything else I am having a hard time with."

"Everything else?"

"Father has always chosen me for tasks such as the one I completed before meeting you because I am able to stay focused and not let anything get in the way. The way you, and even my brother Gabriel are, letting your emotions, the pesky things you feel guide you, I am not that way. I have never been that way and I do not plan on ever being that way."

"You are not answering the question."

"Do you always state the obvious?"

"When I feel that I have to, yes."

"Duly noted."

"I am sorry. Please continue." I am unsure of why I feel the need to apologize, but with as open as he is attempting to be, it seems like the right avenue to take in order to keep him talking. It is obvious that he needs it more than he cares to admit.

"Since my return home, I am unable to escape what happened with Samael. He was my brother you see and for some reason I cannot figure out, letting go is harder this time than it has ever been in the past. I have said goodbye to countless brothers and sisters over the years, yet am unable to do so in this case."

I know what he is getting at but fear bringing it up with him. What he experienced with Samael had caused him to do something he has no familiarity with. It caused him to feel for the first time since his creation and he is having a hard time coping with it. He's right, where Gabriel and I essentially wear our hearts out for everyone to see, Michael is not made to and it is causing him a great deal of pain.

"You understand it so easily…" he whispers and for a moment I am unsure of what he means until I remember what it was I was just thinking about.

"I believe you understand it too. You just cannot accept it because it means that you are not as you appear to be."

"How do I appear to be, assuming little angel?" he asks, his response snide and not at all what I had been expecting. It appears as though the Michael of old is back again. It must mean that I am hitting a little too close to the truth.

"You are a warrior, Michael. You believe that in order to be that and be it effectively that you have to shut off the other parts of you. You do not know any other way of being because you have been living this exact way from the moment of your creation. It is what makes you the pillar of strength that you are."

"How do you know so much about me? Have you and Gabriel been spending that much time together that he has told you everything there is to know about me?"

"This has nothing to do with Gabriel."

"Oh it has everything to do with my brother! This entire mission happened because of him and his annoying attraction to you! You appear to be so bright, yet here you stard, completely stupid."

His words hurt me on a level I did not believe was possible. For whatever reason he has taken what is an innocent friendship between me and his brother and has turned into something cheap and wrong. He knows nothing of the relationship between Gabriel and myself and I refuse to sit here a second longer and listen to him pretend that he does.

Turning my back to him, I make my way over to where Colin still sleeps soundly despite the raised voices and anger that now coat the room. Bending over him, I place a gentle kiss to his brow, the way a mother does to a child and with one final smile for the boy I wanted so desperately to save, I turn and walk from the room.

Michael

This is infuriating.

Colin MacDougall has been healed completely, the light again surrounding him and I am beyond pleased by what has taken place. There is a satisfaction one experiences when they complete a task and I am no different. I am beyond satisfied with the outcome. With everything I experienced with Samael, having to strip him of the light and his life completely, bringing someone back into it is beyond gratifying.

What should have been a moment of celebration has turned into anything but and it is because of the annoying ball of light that has now turned her back and walked away from me.

The way at which she can see so easily into me is disconcerting. Where I have always been able to portray a certain way of being, it is impossible to do with her. She is not privy to my thoughts the way that I am with her and because of that, I believe myself to have some sort of advantage over her, but that is not the case. I am the one at a disadvantage.

There has never been a being alive that is able to get under my skin this way. Even now, with her out of the room, leaving me alone with the sleeping human, she is there, as annoying as ever, just under the surface, pulling at things better left alone. It is just further indication that I should have come here on my own, despite knowing that what I said to her before is true. I would not have been able to reach the boy without her.

Distance is what is needed here, but it is something that until the boy awakens from his slumber, is impossible. We would be here for hours judging by the noises that the young human is making as he sleeps. I am unsure I can handle another five minutes in the angels company, let alone a few hours.

A simple conversation between the two of us has taken such a horrible turn because the more she spoke, the more she reminded me of the brother that was covering for me at home. It was as if he was in the room with us even though he is on a completely different plain than the one we find ourselves on. I could not handle it and as such, began to lose what remained of the calm, collected attitude I had adopted after she caught me thinking about her.

How dare she try to analyze me? A mere ball of light knows nothing of me and what I have been through. She would be better served remembering her place, both here and at home when we are finally allowed to return, because I will not allow a repeat of what has just taken place between us.

I have never felt so twisted inside. With as angry as I am that she seems to know me better in a few short hours than my brothers do in all of the years we have spent together, I am just as angry with myself for the way I treated her. All she had done was attempt to sympathize with me, something she is known for and I turned it around and made her believe that it was wrong.

It is when her similarity to Gabriel and the moments I have witnessed them sharing rises to the surface that everything takes such an awful turn. For whatever reason, thinking about Gabriel spending any real amount of time with this ball of light bothers me to no end and seeing it so clearly in my mind makes the blood running through the vessels body run hot. I begin experiencing the human act of jealousy and I do not like it one bit.

I cannot act this way, it is unbecoming of a being of my stature. Until the moment I came across her for the first time, the way I have been has never caused me one minute of grief, but now that I have met her, spoken to her, seen her at her most pure, I am experiencing a myriad of sensations that have no business being a part of me at all. I want to rid myself of this angel and everything that comes along with her, yet at the same time desiring to bring her closer to me, exposing everything I keep buried so deep inside.

This needs to be handled. Whatever it is that I am going through as it pertains to this bringer of light that I cannot seem to escape, I need to face it. We have to face it. I refuse to go back home again until we do.

Faith

Removing myself from the situation was supposed to make me feel better, but it is having the opposite effect.

Walking away from Michael, after the harsh words he shouted my way, should have been the end of it but that is not the case at all. Standing out here now, I feel empty. There is something missing yet I have no idea what it could possibly be. It could just be that after being as close to Colin as I have been, experiencing his pain the way I did before Michael worked on him has finally worn me down, but I am having a hard time talking myself into believing that.

No, this has to do with Michael. I noticed it before we turned combative toward one another, but now that I am here alone, leaving him inside with Colin, it is still there. I have been experiencing it since before we even began the trek down here. I put it out of my mind, choosing at the time to focus on what being on Earth would feel like, but it is back now and it refuses to let me go.

There is something taking place between me and the archangel. Whether it is because of what we have gone through together since coming across each other or something unrelated, is irrelevant. It is there and I do not think I can rest until I figure out just what it is. It is taking what should be a happy moment for the both of us and turning it into something much darker.

Michael is conflicted. I was able to pick up on that easily when he began speaking of his time with Samael and all that he has faced since being home. What he does not realize is that because of who I am and the ability I have to empathize, I quite literally felt every bit of his conflict, both external and internal. The pain that to most would only be evident in his eyes upon looking into them, I can feel easily and I do not enjoy it.

For whatever reason, Michael believes he has been created, programmed even, to not feel. For centuries it has served him well as evidenced by everything that he has accomplished both with Father and on his own. The problem is, he still feels, he just keeps it buried better than most can do. I have handled enough humans in my time that have displayed the same things as Michael is now and it is not healthy. The more he runs from the emotions, the experience that feeling something brings, the more he will tear himself apart in the end.

"Faith."

"Not now, Michael. I do believe you have said more than enough."

"That is where we disagree."

"All we do is disagree or have you not noticed that?"

I know I should turn around and face him, but with the sting of his earlier words still fresh, that is the last thing I will do. I do not want to feel whatever it is he is bottling, it is hard enough already.

"We disagree because we are nothing alike."

"Now who is the one stating the obvious?"

"I deserve that."

"What are you doing Michael? I walked away from you for a reason and you chose to leave me alone for a reason, so what has changed that brings you out here now?"

"I do not have an answer for that."

He is lying to me. There is an answer, he just does not want to see or acknowledge it. There is a reason that brought him out here, but because it has to do with feeling something, he will not take the steps needed, instead reverting back to what he has always done and clamming up.

"If you believe there is an answer than please, let me know it because I can assure you, I was not lying to you."

"I do not know the answer, only you know that. When you are ready to admit it to me, you know where to find me, until then, I do believe I want to be alone for a little while longer."

As I again turn to walk away from him, repeating almost the same movements as before, he stops me in my tracks. Reaching his arm out, it comes to rest on my shoulder and it is in that moment that I am completely locked in place.

"Please do not walk away from me again."

This is not the angel from a few minutes ago. The one speaking to me now, he's softer, more open. The pleading way the statement sounds as it falls from his lips speaks to it. Turning toward him, no longer caring how I appear, I say the only words I have left, beyond exasperated with the back and forth between us.

"Then give me a reason to stay."

Sliding his hand down from my arm until his hand is resting on mine, in one fluid motion, he yanks me to him and before I have a chance to react to the violation, he pulls my head up until I am level with his gaze and he presses his lips to mine, giving me exactly what I asked for.

My reason to stay.

Chapter Thirteen

Michael

"What have you done to me?"

My breath is labored, I am having a hard time thinking clearly and the only sensation I feel as I break away from the angel nestled in my arms is a peace of which I have never known. It is not what I wanted to say, but the question is a valid one. Since coming into contact with the bringer of light, I have not been myself and it is time that I get answers.

When she prepared herself to walk away from me, something inside of me broke. I could not let her do it, not again. I am still coming to terms with the way it felt the first time she did it, having it happen again is not acceptable. Reaching out to her may be a mistake but she had not walked away, so it was a mistake that served a purpose. For a reason I cannot figure, I need to keep her close to me. Not doing so, letting her distance herself, pulls at a part of me that I do not wish to acknowledge.

I want to blame this wretched human body and its engrained impulses for my reaction to Faith, but since it has been occurring since before we even chose them, I cannot. It may have been the human way of being that drove me to pull her to me and kiss her in the manner at which I did, but anything else I am experiencing while in her company is on me and me alone. I am the cause for it and I need to get to the bottom of it.

There is truth in her earlier statement. I did have the answer to her question, but I do not want to admit to it. In doing so, it will change me, it will change everything, so I attempted to play dumb. The thing is, with this particular being, I cannot get anything past her. She can see through every charade I may attempt to play. I may understand how to hide the way that I am feeling, put on a show in order to make people believe that everything is one particular way, but with her I do not want to do any of that.

Just a few hours in her company and she is changing my entire way of being.

Unacceptable.

"I did not do anything to you."

"That is where you are wrong. Nothing has been right inside of me since I met you. It stands to reason that you are doing something, even if you are unaware of it."

"You've got a lot of nerve you know that? How dare you accuse me of doing something to you when you are the one that grabbed and violated me!"

"I did nothing of the sort. Your lips were pressed to mine, moving in time with mine. Despite your claims of violation, you wanted that kiss just as badly as I did."

"Yeah, well, you're not the only one that feels as though they have been changed by present company."

I am curious now. Going to her the way I did, I assumed I was the only one experiencing things, but with the way she can look anywhere but at me right now, it speaks to something more. She is as affected by me as I am by her and I do not believe either one of us understands it in the slightest.

"Faith."

"Michael."

"Please do not attempt to be smart with me right now. It is not the time. Tell me what you are experiencing."

"I feel drawn to you even though every second I spend with you frustrates me. As I am sure you can tell by the vessel's reaction, you seem to set every nerve ending I have on fire." She points to her arms and I can see the tiny bumps on her arms, as well as the slight lift to the fine hair that coats it. "I am able to read you easily, as if we are sharing the same body, or at the very least, the same space. That kiss, you are right. I wanted it just as much as you did which is why I responded in kind, but at the same time I want nothing more than to be as far away from you as I can possibly get."

It has not slipped my mind that while we are conversing in this way, she is still tightly locked in my embrace. She has made no move to walk away from me though her words speak to her desire to do just that. As much as I want for her to walk away from me now, distance herself so that I may be able to think clearly again, there is a comfort level having her with me in this way and I do not want to lose it.

She is not the only one that feels drawn. I have to use my power just to be able to look away from her at any given moment, my strength not enough on its own. Whatever is happening to us, it is affecting us and not in a good way. Being this connected to her, it can only bring trouble, of that I am sure.

"This, it cannot happen. I am not sure what this even is, but I do know that it is wrong. What we just did, can never be repeated."

The ache that I felt when she walked away is back again and this time it is even stronger than times past. My words, though truthful are causing me pain to say. It is just further proof that what we did is wrong. Telling the truth should never cause this type of ache.

"It did not feel wrong."

How badly I want to agree with her. She is right, it did not feel wrong. Nothing about being with her feels wrong to me. It is quite the opposite. When I am with her, it seems as though the displacement I have felt since my time with Samael has been lifted and I am myself again, albeit, a different, better version. Having Faith in my arms this way, it is peaceful. The small taste of it that I have had, makes me want more, and that is where it becomes wrong.

"It is of little consequence how it felt. You belong to my brother. I have seen the way he looks at you and I will not be the reason he experiences pain."

"You bring up Gabriel so much, it is almost as if you are using him as an excuse! Gabriel has nothing to do with what just happened between us and I do not belong to anyone."

I want to kiss her again just to erase the pain that her final words bring to the surface inside me. She should belong to me. I want to own her, consume her and those thoughts alone are going to be the very thing that damn me to the same hell as my fallen brother before me. I cannot allow myself to feel, especially not for someone like her.

"Michael, tell me what you really feel. Do not use Gabriel and his supposed feelings for me as an excuse. Speak from your heart. You do have one of those. I do believe it is time you use it."

"I do not feel anything."

"That is a lie."

"You know nothing about me. If you knew half as much as you claim, you would know that I do not lie. Even when it might be in my best interests to do so. I will always tell the truth. It is who I am and what I have been made to be."

"Evading the question, explaining it away. You are as good at those as you are at lying. If you will not tell me what you feel than please just tell me what you are thinking."

"You want to know what I feel so badly! I feel as though you have put a spell on me, something that if Father ever found out about, you would be removed from Heaven for. I cannot think straight when I am within two feet of you. All I see is you. In a short period of time, you have completely consumed my being and nothing else seems to matter to me, but having you as close to me as you are now. Kissing you was a selfish move and one that despite knowing it is wrong, I want to do again, repeatedly. I despise every bit of this experience and I want nothing more than for it to be over."

Even knowing what my words will do to her, I am taken aback when she backs away and removes my arms from around her body. While she is doing everything I have asked of her, the emptiness I am met with once she is completely separated is almost more than I can stand. Why of all beings in Heaven am I the one going through this now? Why must it be me that experiences the highs and lows that seem to come along with partnering with a bringer of light?

Colin needs to wake up so that we can check on him and return home. The more time spent around her now, especially in the body that she possesses will only make what has happened that much worse. I meant what I said to her, I do not enjoy one second of this and it has nothing to do with being something new. I am open to trying new things, but in this case, I cannot be. She has the power to change me and that just cannot come to pass.

I am a warrior of Heaven and a warrior I shall stay. Feelings, emotions, they will never be a part of who I am, and neither will Faith.

Faith

I have been fighting it since the moment I laid eyes on him. I felt the shift in Heaven and did nothing about it. If I had just brought this up then, maybe none of this would be happening now.

Kissing Michael was unexpected but the moment our lips met, we connected. It is that connection that is driving him now. I can see it plain as day. He is afraid of what the two of us being together will mean. For the first time in his existence it appears as though he is frightened by something because he has no control over it. That is what it is all about for him. Control.

Michael needs the control that being a warrior of Heaven brings. He knows what to expect and he plans his movements around it accordingly. With me, he cannot do that and it scares him. It is hard for me to believe, only having humans to base it off of, but it appears as though he is a creature of habit. Routine. He needs those things in order to function and kissing me, it is not routine and he is struggling with everything he has in order to bring it all back together.

I am not sure if he is aware, but when we kissed, his light, my light, our light, it came together as one singular entity. I opened my eyes only for a split second before Michael pulled away and it was then that I witnessed it. He may believe it to be wrong, he may even be deathly afraid of it, but the way our light connected together, that is what makes it so right.

He despises the way that he feels and while hearing it hurts me on a level I am not quite familiar with, I also understand it. Just because it feels right does not mean that I am accepting of it. I am much like him in that I do not understand the pull that is taking place between us, what makes me so in tune with him. I also wish it would cease, at least until such time as I can sort out what is really going on, but it appears that we are not that lucky. I am more accepting of it because any attempt I make at pushing it away only makes things worse.

Why he feels the need to bring Gabriel into this, I may never understand, but he has to realize that Gabriel is not the one that is here with me now and he is most definitely not the one that I kissed back so willingly. Nor would he ever be. While the archangel and I may see eye to eye on a lot of things, I do not believe we are destined to be together. I do not see myself with him. When I close my eyes, especially now in this human form, it is not the soft hearted angel I see, but Michael.

Saying I belong to someone is offensive to my sensibilities. I refuse to believe that I am owned by anyone other than my father. He is the one that created me and as such, my way of being, my whole reason for being here at all is to serve and love him. I do not belong nor will I ever to another being, human or celestial in nature and any mention to the contrary turns my insides out. There is a flaw in my way of thinking though and it is one that try as I might, I cannot ignore.

I want to belong to Michael.

For whatever reason, he has gotten to me and I am unable to shake him even when I take steps to distance myself. Just as I see him when I close my eyes, clear as the light of home in my mind, I also see us together, being owned by each other so completely. The way I feel is disconcerting, maybe even a little frightening but that is where him and I differ. He wants nothing more than for it to be over, and I want nothing more than for it to begin.

"Why does it hurt when you distance yourself from me?"

"I do not have the answer to that, Michael. I do believe that is something only you can answer."

In the few seconds of silence after I have spoken, I notice he has bridged the gap between us again, taking steps toward me instead of away the way I have been expecting. If he is so against this, then why bring himself deeper into it?

"I cannot do this with you, yet I cannot bring myself to turn away."

"There is a simple solution if only you open your eyes enough to see it."

"What would that be?"

"Do not turn away from it. Embrace whatever is driving you, Michael. When we arrived here, you told me to do something if things became too much. Do you remember what it was that you said?"

"Yes, I remember it vividly."

"I suppose it now my turn to say the same in return. Believe in me; trust in me, but most of all, do not turn away from it, no matter how frightening it is for you."

"That is easier said than done. What is taking place here, what has already taken place, Faith, if Father ever learned of it, we would both pay the ultimate price. I am sure by now you are aware how important my position is to me and I am more than a little aware of your feelings as well. What we are experiencing is not worth losing everything."

"Then what do you suggest we do?"

"Finish what we started, go home and go our separate ways. Faith, no matter how right it felt embracing you the way I did, kissing you even more so, it can never happen again. It is not worth the price I would pay. The price we would pay. Your place is with my brother and it always will be."

Chapter Fourteen

Michael

There was this moment as I came through the gates, Faith by my side that I expected to see the very disappointed face of Father waiting for me. With no immediate contact occurring between us and Gabriel during our time on the planet, I could only assume what would be awaiting us when we arrived back home.

What I had expected to see was not there to greet us. We arrived home to no fanfare whatsoever, which seemed to put Faith at ease, but did not do the same for me. If Father was not here now to greet us, then it meant there would surely be a meeting or two in the future where he would let the both of us know just how disappointed he was with what we had done.

Even garnering another soul for the light the way we did would not save us from whatever punishment he sees fit to give. It is not that he would overlook all we had done, because he would indeed be pleased that we had brought another soul back where it belongs and even more so away from my fallen brother Lucifer, but it would not excuse the steps we had taken in order to get there. The rules that we had broken.

We would most definitely be paying for that.

Not much has been said between us since our last discussion on Earth and even though I stand by all that I did say, I cannot help but wonder what she is thinking about. If she agrees with what I believe is the right thing and if she will ever utter another word to me again. I know I said I wanted to go our separate ways once we had made our way home, I just did not expect it to feel quite this lonely.

I would prefer another sparring match with the bringer of light over the silent treatment I have been receiving. Does she not realize that I am doing this for the betterment of both of us? That despite the way being near her feels, it is much safer for the both of us being apart?

"Thank you for doing everything you did for Colin. I am glad that we were able to reach him in time and change his path."

It is the first words she has spoken in what has surely been hours and even though it is not much, I cannot let them be the final ones shared between us. I need to say more, continue the conversation, despite knowing that letting her go her own way is the right thing to do.

"You do not have to thank me. It is what I am here to do."

She breaks off of the path we have been taking and as I watch her turn away, her back now to me, I reach out to stop her.

"Faith…"

"Yes Michael?" she asks turning back to again face me.

"About what happened down there—I feel as though I need to say something."

"There is nothing left to say. You made your position very clear before and I have heard and accepted it."

"While everything I said to you previously stands, I need to make sure you understand it as well as accept it."

"What more is there to accept? There is something taking place between us, it is causing us to act in ways that neither of us are familiar with and it is most uncomfortable. It is that which caused us to kiss. I understand your position and you do not have to worry about me speaking about it to anyone here. It will remain our secret."

There is a moment as she alludes to keeping what happened between us a secret where I feel myself becoming angry. Quickly shaking it off, not wanting her to witness how bothered I am by her statement, I focus my attention on what still needs to be said. For all of her supposed understanding, she does not get my position at all. In fact, what she believes is false.

"I am under the impression with as quiet as you have been with me since leaving Colin that you believe I regret what took place between us. I want to be sure as we go our separate ways that you are aware of the truth. I do not regret kissing you. I admit that what I am experiencing is new to me and I do not believe it to be right, but I do not regret it in the slightest."

"Nor do I." she says in response, though her tone is clipped and cold, a side of her I have yet to witness and am quite confused by.

"You will see, when we have had time apart, things will go back to the way they were before we were brought together for this undertaking together. We will go back to our lives and it will be as if this never happened."

"And what if I do not wish for it to be that way?"

There is a pull in my chest at her question and a warm sensation coating it, again, things I have no experience with but am unable to disregard. Whatever the connection is with this angel, it is bringing things to life inside of me that are better off buried.

Her place is with Gabriel and the question she asks just proves it. He would know the right response to this, where I am at a complete loss. I have never dealt with something of this nature before and am not looking forward to doing so now.

"It is the way that it has to be."

"You never explained why to me. I want to know. You seem so sure that anything occurring between us is wrong and if I am to move on from the way I am feeling the way you claim I need to, then I do believe you owe me an explanation."

"I know nothing of loving another. I was created with a clear purpose and it is one that I will follow through on for the rest of eternity, with little time for much else. I love Father with everything that I have and because of that, no matter what we feel for one another, or what is taking place between us, I can never give you what you need."

"What is it that you think I need?"

"I cannot speak to what you need, but I can tell you what I believe you deserve if that will help?"

She nods her head but her eyes turn away from mine, almost as if she is giving me permission to tell her things, but is most unwilling to accept what I will eventually say.

"Please look at me."

When she does not do as I have asked of her, the ever present ache in my chest pulls at me again. With my position here, I am quite used to other beings bending to my will, doing as I ask and not questioning me or my motives in the slightest, but with her, it is the complete opposite. Where before I would have found it infuriating, now it just hurts.

"Faith, in a short period of time, I have come to see what makes you who you are. The reason Father chose you to be a bringer of light. You deserve someone who can love you unconditionally, openly and proudly. Someone who has enough room in their heart for not only our Father but for all that you are as well."

"And you believe that person to be your brother."

"I do not believe it, I know it. Gabriel is everything that I am not, nor can I ever be."

Pushing this angel in the direction of my brother is tearing me apart inside. I want so badly to claim her as my own, based purely on everything I have been through with her in our short time together, but what I have told her rings true. I cannot give her what she needs and deserves. Gabriel can. Despite what I want, what I may or may not feel, I need to do the right thing.

Focusing on the way all of this is making me feel, I do not notice right away that she has moved and is closer to me now, our bodies a mere step away from becoming one with each other again, much the way they did as I held her on the planet hours before. It is only when she reaches for my hand, locking it with hers that I see it.

Bright as the very sky above us, is our light, but instead of being two singular rays, they have come together and melded into one, something that as long as I have been alive, I have never once bared witness too.

"You can believe all you want that Gabriel is the one for me and that what we shared, what we still continue to share is wrong, but this, what is happening between us, Michael, this cannot be denied. This means something and I will not rest until I know what that is."

"I need to go."

"You mean, you need to run."

"I am doing no such thing. I do not run from anything."

"Prove it."

I have been in countless battles, both of strength and will and have always been able to keep my wits about me, but standing here now, being pushed by her, the way at which she states for me to prove it, an almost teasing lilt to her voice, I have had more than I can stand. If proof is what she is after, I am more than willing to oblige her.

Breaking my hand from hers and wrapping it around her body, I pull her into mine, until we are so close it appears as though we are one being and I crash my lips down onto hers, the desire for more ever present the second we meet. Where I expect her to tense, or back away, she does not and instead parts her lips, the smallest breath of air escaping as she does.

Frozen still in the moment, the feel of her breath on my lips as she awaits my next move, I think about what I am doing and what it means. I can stop this now, push her away, go my own way and never have to see her again or I can respond to the heat building inside of me, the desire to taste her fully overriding the most rational parts of my brain and drown myself in the feel of her.

It is not an easy choice to make, but before I am able to make it, she takes my choice away as she runs her tongue across my bottom lip, bringing her lips back to mine and capturing them, sucking ever so gently. It is in that moment that all rational thought ceases to exist and I allow the drowning to begin.

Faith

It had been my hope that when we arrived back, we would go our separate ways and I could use the time alone in order to process everything that had taken place between Michael and I. As I prepared to break away from him though, I realized I could not walk away without thanking him for everything he had done.

He did not have to help me with Colin. He could have gotten a look at the boy before venturing down to save him and decided he was not worth the time or effort, but he had not done it and for that needed to be thanked. I knew it was a risk given the growing feelings I am having toward him, but I could not let it end this way.

What should have been a simple thank you and goodbye, turned quickly into so much more. Something happened when he began explaining himself to me. Hearing him say that he did not regret what happened between us, it broke something inside of me. Where I had spent the remaining time we shared together quiet, it was as if a dam had broken open and I could finally speak again.

The idea of his that Gabriel is better suited for me because he can give me what I deserve is so ludicrous it is almost funny. Michael has no idea what I want, need or deserve and for him to make assumptions about it just pushed me even further. What I experience when I am with him, while new to me is something I want to learn more about, not shy away from. I would not agree with what he wanted of me because I wanted so much more.

Showing him how our light connects was a calculated move on my part. I did not believe him to be aware of it, as he had not had his eyes open the last time it happened and before I walked away, I wanted to show him just what he would be giving up. His reaction did not come as a surprise. It is easy to see when Michael is not in control, his first inclination is to walk away and this time, I was not about to let him.

Pushing him further, testing him was not part of any plan, it was just a natural response to what he had said before. I expected him to blow it off, break all contact between us, especially with as uncomfortable as he became the minute he saw our light joining together but he did the complete opposite.

Now we find ourselves locked in an embrace, at a proverbial point of no return. I can sense the conflict inside of him, which is why before he has a chance to do the honorable thing and pull away, I pull him closer, craving him so completely that I tease him first with my tongue and then with my lips as I suck on his. It is then that his body goes lax, though still maintaining a firm hold on me and I know he is completely mine.

It is only when he begins to kiss me back, responding to my earlier tasting with a taste of his own that I hear the clearing of a throat behind me and it brings the desire coursing through me to a complete standstill.

I have no idea who could be standing behind me, but just the thought of it being Father, when Michael is already of the belief that what we are doing together is wrong, ties me up in knots. We are both frozen in place now, our lips barely touching, neither one of us willing to be the first to completely break away.

Michael breaks first, his arms releasing their hold from around my body, but not before bringing his lips to mine again, barely brushing against them and whispering the name of the person he now knows is standing directly behind me, sending a shiver down my spine.

"Gabriel..."

His eyes meet mine for a brief second and I can see that he has taken my response in the wrong way. Where he believes me to have shivered because of the name he whispered, I am reacting instead to the way his lips felt as they brushed against mine whispering it. As eagerly as I want to correct him, with Gabriel standing behind us, I know it is impossible.

"I am happy to see the two of you have arrived home in one piece."

Michael turns from me and I want to scream at him the moment he does. There is an emptiness in my chest now that was not there the entire time we were standing in close proximity to each other and I desperately want it to be that way again. With him standing beside me, I feel put together, in a manner of speaking, whole.

"Brother, if I had feelings, I might be offended at your lack of faith in my abilities."

I watch as Gabriel laughs and I cannot help feeling uncomfortable with the exchange. It is not only because it feels as though I am interrupting a brotherly exchange, but also because of what is said. Any mention of Michael and feeling is a little too close for comfort. It is the very reason there seems to be this back and forth between us.

"When I heard that you had returned, I felt it imperative to come directly to you. I had no idea I would be interrupting something. Faith," he says, turning to face me, the smile still evident across his face. "My apologies for just popping in on you that way."

"You have nothing to apologize for, brother. You did not interrupt anything of importance."

"Michael—"

"It is okay, Gabriel. I am sure it is only a matter of time before Father pays me a visit. I do believe I will leave you both alone and return to my post."

Before either angel can say anything in response, I disappear, making sure as I do that neither of them sees the tears as they begin to fall from my eyes.

Michael

What has just taken place is exactly why I said that she would be better off with my brother. Where I had just said the first thing that came to mind, Gabriel seemed to sympathize with her and realize my mistake instantly. He is proving himself to be much more worthy of her time and affection then I am.

"Michael, you know I do not normally question the decisions you make as they pertain to your own business, but in this case I feel I must. Surely you think more of what I witnessed appearing here than you claim."

"It is not of import, brother."

"I believe it is of the utmost importance."

I am aware that I brought this conversation on myself in acting the way I did, but it does not mean I have to stand here and listen to it a moment longer than I already have. Especially coming from who is behind it. I do not need further reminders of how I do not measure up.

"Just speak your peace Gabriel, so that we may move on from this and get to the real reason for your visit."

"What is going on between you and Faith?"

"Nothing."

"So walking in on the two of you locked in a very tight embrace, your lips pressed together in what appears to be a kiss, is what we are calling nothing these days?"

"She was just thanking me for all that I did during our time below. Do not make it out to be more scandalous than it is."

"I realize that because you were created before me, it makes you a big brother of sorts and therefore more knowledgeable than me, but if you expect me to sit here and believe that drivel you are spouting as truth, you are sadly mistaken. So, let me ask you again. What is going on between you and the bringer of light?"

"It is complicated and I am not quite sure I can give you an answer that will appease your rabid curiosity."

"Why don't you try?"

I am left facing two choices in the moment. I can either remain tight lipped as it pertains to what I am experiencing with Faith, which will only mean I will have to answer for it later with Father, or I can tell Gabriel all there is to know and hopefully gain some insight into the human condition at the same time, as it appears that whatever is taking place between Faith and myself is human in nature.

"You know the way I am. How I have always been. This angel, she reaches beyond that way of being and touches me in ways I am most unfamiliar and uncomfortable with. I am drawn to her in a way that I cannot even find the adequate words to describe and when we touch—"

"There is a connection?" Gabriel offers up so easily, almost as if it is something I should have known all along.

"Yes, but Gabriel, it is more than just a connection. I witnessed something with her earlier that I am unaware is even possible."

"Do you want to elaborate on that?"

"She placed her hand into mine and the minute we connected our individual lights, they became one. As bright as I have seen a light shine, the combined version was infinitely more powerful."

He seems lost in thought after my explanation, but before I can ask him what he believes this might be, he lips rise into a smile, almost as if he knows something that I do not and finds it amusing. It is not often he is more knowledgeable than I am, but it is not completely unheard of either. In this instance it appears as though he has the answers I need in order to put all of this into perspective.

"Gabriel, if you have any information about this, now is the time to share it."

"I cannot believe you have not pieced it together yourself. Michael, I have known what is going on since before the two of you left home. If you had only focused on that which you have been taught and less on how wrong you perceive it to be, you would already have your answer."

"Brother, I do not have the patience to go round and round with you, especially not about this. Will you please share your knowledge with me before I lose what is left of my already dwindling sanity and do something to you I might later regret?"

Gabriel laughs loudly, the sound bubbling up from deep inside of him. It is in watching him react this way that I am again reminded of just how different we are even though we are made of the very same fiber. Where he can express his emotions easily, I am locked in place, unable to even express the most basic of feeling.

"You would never dream of hurting a hair on my head, Michael. Your threat has nothing behind it, but I do believe it is time I put you out of your misery."

""I am sure you are just chomping at the bit for that. So what is it that you know that I have yet to learn?"

"Michael, you are reacting to Faith in the manner at which you are because she is something more than just a bringer of light. In fact, there is no being in creation more important to you than her."

"And that makes her what exactly?"

"That is quite easy brother. It makes her your beloved."

Chapter Fifteen

Faith

There are times when being as emotional as I am can be a good thing. When reaching out to a particularly hard and distrusting human for instance. Showing the right amount of emotion, having it be real and not imagined or faked can be the very thing that stands between me saving or losing them.

Sure, there are times where it can be a hindrance and the sheer magnitude of whatever emotion I am feeling at the time so powerful that I want nothing more to escape it, but I would never think of following through. It is as much a part of who I am as the light is here in Heaven.

Hearing Michael's words, seeing the truth of his statement in his eyes as he tells his brother that what he interrupted meant nothing to him, the emotions I experienced, were enough to make me want to flee. I wanted nothing more in that moment than to disappear, hide away inside of myself and never come out again. If the way I am is so great, why does it hurt so badly?

I know I think differently than him. I am aware that my perception of what is taking place between us is on the lighter side of things. I can only see the good from it, whereas Michael sees all of the things that can go wrong by us joining in any capacity. I have tried to make him see things differently, but it appears as though Gabriel was right in the way he explained his brother to me. Michael is very set in his ways and the only one that can ever change his mind on any given topic is Michael himself. He will not allow it to be any other way.

Which means everything that I feel for him, the way our light joins together and becomes one entity whenever we touch, I have to bottle all of that and move on from it. I have to give him what he wants because there is no amount of explaining, showing that I can do that will turn him around from the road he has put himself on. He will forever look at the two of us as something wrong, when the reality is, even if Heaven does not agree with what is taking place between us, the strength of our lights as they come together proves that it is right.

Something that powerful could never be wrong.

"What you are going through Faith, Heaven does not look down on or believe it is wrong. Nor do I."

When I left my place with Michael and Gabriel, I had come straight back to my post. I knew it was only a matter of time before Father found his way to me and I wanted to use the free time I did have to get back into the swing of things. I wanted to look in on all my charges, making sure that my time away did not harm them in any way. It had not been that long, yet apparently, Father knows no timetable, for here he stands, majestic as always.

"If Heaven is not against what is taking place than why does Michael believe it to be so wrong?"

"I do believe that somewhere deep inside your mind, you know the answer to that question, so I do not feel I need to answer it."

"And if I don't?"

"You may doubt the validity of what you believe to be the answer, but that does not mean that you do not know it. Look inside yourself, Faith. The answers to everything as it pertains to Michael are there. You just need to allow yourself to see it."

When the Almighty appears before you and tells you to do something, it is always in your best interests to do it, but there is something about his tone this time that tells me it is not something he is forcing me to do, but something that he wishes I would do just for the knowledge to be had from it.

Doing as he requests, I think about everything I know about the archangel. There is not really a lot that I am aware of, but the things I do know center around one core belief system.

Michael believes himself to be a warrior and as such cannot imagine himself being any other way then he has been since his creation. The mere thought of change in that regard alone is enough to send him running in the other direction. I have witnessed all of this during my time with him. He is not against change, but only on his terms.

Father is right, I do have the answer.

"He believes it to be wrong because it is something that he has no control over."

"Yes, that is precisely it. What the two of you are going through, it has a name. It has been around as long as time. I am the one that brought it into existence before I created Michael and the others. He has been made aware of it since his creation, but it appears as though the passage of time has made him doubt its authenticity."

"So, like me, he knows the answer, but is refusing to see it?"

"Precisely."

"If I ask you to explain what you know, are you going to tell me that I already know the answer?"

He smiles and whatever nervousness had begun to grow inside of me at questioning him is quickly abated and I am again put at ease.

"You do not know the answer to this because it is something that you have never been told about. I have no doubt you have heard tales during your time here, but that is all they are. Folklore, stories without fact. I do believe it is time that I inform you of everything."

"I do not mean this with any degree of disrespect, but if he is so unwilling to see it, does it matter what this is between us? It is not as if anything will ever come of it anyway."

"That is where you are wrong. Faith, you are Michael's beloved. You are everything that he is not, yet everything he aspires to be deep inside of himself. He may be too stubborn to see it, but the way you are, is what he longs to be and with the bond now making itself apparent between you two, I do believe that one day in the future, he will become that very being. He will be complete."

Beloved. I have heard talk about it, though I have to admit that I never put much thought into what was being said. It never had any bearing on the work that I am expected to do here, so I had heard it and put it out of my mind. It appears now though, that I should have listened more when it first came around, because now I am the one experiencing it firsthand.

"Does that also mean that he is what I aspire to be?"

"Yes. The thoughts you were having before I arrived, wanting to be different than the way you had been created, feeling less than you do, that is happening because of the bond."

"So, I aspire to be more like Michael? Surely you can see how wrong that is. He is cold, callous and has no regard for anyone's feelings. He places all of his time and attention into being a warrior for you, which is not a bad thing, but is nothing at all like what I wish to be."

"You are correct in your train of thought. You do not aspire to be exactly the way Michael presents himself, but there are aspects of him that you want."

"Like what?"

"His strength. His ability to see a task through to the end, never letting himself get taken off track until it is complete. Those are the aspects that you wish for yourself. If you want proof of that, you only need to look at the undertaking the two of you went on together. Michael, seeing your struggle with the human took it upon himself to head down there, in order to handle what you could not."

Father is telling the truth. I have wished to be stronger, so that I do not have to call on others to help me in certain situations. Michael being able to do what he did on the planet, saving Colin in the way he did, it is exactly what I want to do myself.

"What else can you tell me about the connection between us?" I ask, taking the attention off the realization I have made and back onto something I can garner answers from. "I have seen our individual lights meld together, is that common?"

"Yes. The bond that the two of you share, being beloved, it will continue to present itself to you in that manner. It wants to bring the two of you together in any way possible. That is why, when you two embraced earlier, it felt as though you were one singular being instead of two separate ones. The two of you together, are more powerful than you are separately."

"He will never see this as anything more than an annoyance."

"That is where you are wrong. For all of the parts of Michael that make him a stubborn angel, he is not against seeing the truth. It will just take him longer than it would his other siblings."

"You are aware he believes that Gabriel is the one meant for me, are you not?"

He laughs again and I find myself joining in with him. It appears as though I am not the only one that believes Michael's thought process to be entertaining. As wonderful as Gabriel is, how alike we are, it does not a love connection make. He can believe I am meant to be with his brother all he wants, but the truth of the matter is in my very real reaction to him.

"As you well know, I am aware of everything. In this particular instance, I have to admit it is quite entertaining. Michael is well aware of how the beloved bond works, so believing Gabriel to be the one is amusing. Gabriel's time will come, it has been written already, but it is not with you."

Hearing that Gabriel will experience what I am now going through sparks a mixed reaction in me. I want him to find his happiness, of that there is no doubt, but to feel the things I am now, I would never wish that on my worst enemy. I would not wish it on Lucifer and every being alive is aware of how evil he is. It is too much to handle for even the strongest being, something I am learning with each day that passes. The up and down of it all is nauseating.

"It only appears that way for you because of who you are connected to, Faith."

"You mean the others that will experience this will have it easier?"

"Not easier, but it will be different. You are struggling with this because it is with Michael. You have spent a good amount of time with him as of late, surely you can see the truth in my statement."

He is right about that. Trying to break through Michael's stubbornness is akin to running into a brick wall repeatedly. The only gift given in the end being that of a splitting headache.

"Faith, never change. The way you think amuses me to no end. There is no better match for Michael than you, of that I am sure."

As much as I want to grasp onto his compliment, I know that explaining the beloved bond to me is not the only reason for his visit. I am more than a little aware of the rules I have broken going to Colin and I have no doubt he is here now to go over that with me, and decide in the end on a fitting punishment. I only hope that in the end, doing what I have done does not leave me with the same end result as Lucifer.

I want to continue helping people from the comfort of home, despite going against that very home and the creator of it in order to save a human.

"The reason for my visit, as you have already surmised, has to do with the adventure the two of you went on, but the place you have allowed your mind to go dear child, that is where you have been misled. I am not here to punish you, or to have you removed from Heaven."

"Then what happens to me?"

"We will get to that, but first I want you to start from the beginning and explain everything to me. What lead up to you making the decision to go to Earth, and also what happened from the moment you touched down. In order for me to truly understand what has taken place, I need to have all the information at my disposal."

"I thought you were aware of everything already?"

"It is no secret that I am the seer of all things, but what most do not realize is that I do not make decisions based purely on what I have seen or what I know. I make them after time spent speaking to the people involved, which I am now here to do with you."

I feel the guilt building in me as he speaks. I have questioned him and then from those questions made my own assumptions to the way he is and I am now being proven wrong. He may be the seer of all things, the very being that created all of the beauty I am now surrounded by, but he was still a being that felt and experienced just as I do and judging him on what I have heard, or come to figure on my own as the truth is wrong.

"You have every right to question and make your own assumptions and conclusions, Faith. I am merely stating facts. I am here now to hear your side of what has taken place and from there I will decide the best course of action moving forward."

It is time. I am going to tell him everything that he wishes to know and no matter what the end result, I would accept it and move forward in the best way possible, even if I had to earn his faith and trust in me back.

I would not fail him again.

Chapter Sixteen

Michael

The beloved bond. Now I know my brother is playing a trick on me. After all the time that has passed since Father first spoke of it, surely he realizes that it does not actually exist and is only a pretty fable he wanted to fill our heads with while we were learning everything we would need in order to serve him to the best of our ability.

According to what we have been told, there are two bonds in existence that are so powerful nothing is able to tear them apart. First, there is the soul-mate bond. One complete soul, split apart and forced to wander the earth for multiple lifetimes until finally coming together as one being again when the time is right. The other bond, is the one of the beloved. Two separate beings, brought together through their differences. The beloved would be all that we are not. In coming together, the areas at which we are weak on our own, we are now strengthened by. It is a connection so deep that just as the soul-mates will eventually come together as one, the beloved are connected at all times.

This is what Gabriel is trying to make me believe in and it is amusing because he is not earning the desired response in me. There is no way that the bringer of light is my beloved. It is just not possible. If she is to be what I aspire to be, then it appears as though Father made a mistake since she has nothing that I would want.

"Even now, knowing that it is the truth I am speaking, you are still refusing to see it."

"There is nothing to see, Gabriel. As you have clearly seen by invading my thoughts in the manner you have, Faith has no qualities that I want. I do not aspire to be like her in any way. Therefore, what you believe to be the truth is false."

"I want to be wrong about this, believe me, but I am not. Faith is your beloved and if you would do as the humans say and pull your head out of your ass, you would see it."

"Your time on the planet is changing you brother. You know how Father feels about you speaking that way."

"I am sure Father will overlook it in this instance, but do not change the subject. You know I am telling you the truth about this, so why are you fighting so hard against it?"

"Because it is ludicrous. We were created to love one being. Our father. Stepping away from that and feeling for another goes against everything that is right."

"Father is the very one that created the bond to begin with. Do you really believe he would have brought it into existence at all if it was so wrong? Michael, he wants you to experience this and not only that, but experience it with Faith. She is everything you are not and even a blind man can see it."

"You are wrong. I do not wish to feel as she does. In fact, I would rather jab my own eyes out with my sword than feel half of what that bringer of light does."

"Stubborn ass—"

He cuts himself off before finishing the statement but I cannot help laughing at his discomfort. He is watching his language because of where he is, but there is no doubt that he believes me to be exactly what he has just attempted to call me. It is not the first time I have heard people speak of me in this way and I am sure it will not be the last. I will gladly accept being labeled stubborn when it happens because I refuse to believe every single thing that is thrown before me.

"You tell me that you are experiencing things with her that you cannot make logical sense of, becoming one with her, unable to think clearly when in her presence, yet you deny that all of what you are going through is exactly what happens when one finds their beloved. Think about what Father told us, Michael."

"Even if I do as you say and accept this as fact, what difference does it make? So Heaven will not frown upon it. It still does not make it right for me. I cannot let a bond such as the one you are describing override my way of being. I am not made to love and cherish anyone other than Father. I am a warrior."

"You are more than a warrior, Michael."

"That is where we disagree. Standing by Father's side, fighting alongside him and the rest of you, that is what I was made for. There is no room for what being a beloved entails."

"Even if the bond between the two of you makes you a better warrior for Heaven?"

"It will not do that, Gabriel. Do you not see? Being bonded to this angel, it will open me up in ways that will expose me to our enemies as weak. That is not a risk I am willing to take. If I were to begin feeling now and Lucifer caught wind of it, it would surely bring about my true death."

"You not accepting this as fact will be the thing that brings about your true death. Your stubbornness will be the very thing that takes you from us. Of that I am sure. If you want to be the best warrior you can be, the way that you claim, than you need to open your eyes, see this for what it is, embracing it now before it is too late and you are unable to be saved."

"I will never accept this."

"What if I were to tell you that I find myself in love with Faith? That I would like nothing more than to bring her to me, never letting her go for the rest of eternity. Connecting with her in every physical and emotional way possible until both of us are dizzy from the love and passion we feel for one another? How would that make you feel?"

What Gabriel is attempting to do, it is getting to me. As he speaks of doing anything remotely physical with her, I feel my body tense and it takes a great deal of power to contain the urge inside of me to rip him limb from limb. It is in experiencing this primal reaction to his words that I start to see everything he has been saying.

As much as I want to deny the facts, I cannot do it any longer. Faith is my beloved and there will never be another being in existence that will place their hands on her but me. I will never allow it. I do not even need to bear witness to anything taking place to know that. The way her body felt melding to mine when we held each other, I never want to be without, nor do I want another man or angel experiencing it. They would never survive it.

I would destroy them all.

"Mission accomplished."

"You act as though I did not know the intent behind your words. You have never been good at getting things past any of us Gabriel, I do not understand why you continue to try."

"I was not attempting to get anything past you. I was merely trying to awaken the truth inside you and if I do say so myself, I did a masterful job. I can tell you now see what I have been trying to tell you. She is yours, Michael. She always has been."

"It does not change the facts, Gabriel."

"What facts would you be alluding to? I have already told you that Heaven will look on it favorably, as will our Father since he is the reason you are experiencing it to begin with. What else can there be?"

"I cannot give her what she needs."

"Not this again!" he shouts and I can tell by the shaking of his head that he is not only annoyed with the way I am acting but disappointed as well. "You are the only one that believes yourself unworthy Michael and quite frankly it is getting old."

"Can you stand there and tell me that she would not be better suited with someone like you? As hard as it was for me to hear you allude to doing things to her, I cannot deny that with you, she would have everything she could ever want, need or desire."

"When are you going to open your eyes? She does not want me. If the look in her eyes that I witnessed when I appeared earlier is any indication, the one she wants to experience her desires with is standing before me now, most unwilling to give it to her."

"What is that supposed to mean? What did you witness from her earlier, because what I saw, is not at all the way you describe it. Hearing your name, it did things to her."

"Michael, when I arrived earlier, it was to ask you about the mission, but the more I stand here and speak with you, I am finding myself growing increasingly bored because what you think, it is not even close to the reality of the situation around you. Her reaction was not to my name, but to the way you said it as you held her. Clearly Father did not bless with you with god given sense when he created you."

Could what Gabriel is saying be true? Could I have misread the situation and she had been reacting to me all along? With my earlier words about her floating around heavily in the mind, the entire time I have stood here conversing with my brother, I can only feel as though I have made an already bad situation that much worse. Not only had I said unforgiveable things, pushing her away from me, but I had misread her on top of it. If we are to be as connected as the beloved bond states, how is that even possible?

"Before you yell at me for invading your thoughts again, I do believe I have the answer to that question."

"Well, you have wasted no time making your point known before, so please, tell me now."

"You being as unaccepting as you have been has closed you off from being able to truly connect with her the way that you should be. She has connected to you, but is being met with a proverbial brick wall as it were."

"Even if I accept that as fact, what am I supposed to do about all of this now? I have pushed her away, surely after the way I acted earlier she will want nothing to do with me."

"There is only one way to find out. Go to her, Michael and for heaven's sakes, make it right."

Faith

When I pictured explaining everything that has taken place to Father, I always imagined him being upset with me, stripping me of my position and eventually casting me out. It may have been wrong to take it in such a dramatic direction, but having no experience in going against him before, it was the only place my mind would allow me to go.

What I am experiencing now as I have told him all that I can about my time both in Heaven and below with Michael is the complete opposite of all of that. He stands intently listening, his eyes never wavering from mine as I open myself up to his mercy. There are even moments throughout where he appears intrigued by what I have been through. I want nothing more than to ask him what he is thinking, but the fear I have regarding what his final decision will be regarding my punishment stops me.

I trust in his earlier words regarding my fate. I do not believe I will be removed from Heaven, but there can be no denying that I went against him and there has to be repercussions to that. I will have no other choice but accept them, whatever they may be, but it does not quell the fear buried inside me. I do not want this happening at all.

"If you had been given an available option in handling Colin from Heaven, would you have still travelled down to the planet or would you have handled it from here?"

"I would have handled it from home. I am aware of the rules as it pertains to us leaving and the last thing I wanted to do was go against them, and you."

"Would you like to know why I made that rule to begin with?"

There is a lot of talk that happens here, angels attempting to understand Father and his motivations. I have never been a part of it, but I have heard a great deal and a lot of the chatter seems to center around trying to figure out why he does some of the things he does. If he is willing to open up to me in this way, allowing me to see his way of thinking, there is no way I will turn away from it. Of course I want to know more.

"I can only assume it was put in place as a safety measure."

"You would not be wrong. When a being such as yourself takes a vessel, your light remains but not much else. Where Raphael, Gabriel, Michael and Uriel are able to maintain their power, it does not work the same way with the others. The rule was put in place to protect you so that you do not find yourself stuck in a situation that could bring about your death. Faith, when an angel passes, they cease to exist. That is not an end I want any of you to reach, which is why it hurt me deeply to see you disregard it so easily."

"I did not do it to hurt you. I just wanted to do right by the boy. It is what you appointed me to do after all."

"That I did. It is knowing that, and seeing just how brightly the light burns in you, the goodness that you can bring the world that I do believe I have come up with an adequate solution to the issue."

"What would that be?"

"A change of position. I do not believe that you should be punished for the steps that you took in order to bring another person back into the light. That would defeat the purpose of what I am trying to accomplish. In doing what you have done, I do believe that a change of position is appropriate. You can be utilized to your full potential."

"What position did you have in mind?"

"I wish for you to stand by my side." He says smiling as I take in the gravity of what he has just laid out before me. "In doing so, I believe it will not only help in your own personal growth, but mine as well. It has been far too long since I have surrounded myself with pure emotion."

"You want me to stand—beside you?" I ask, my voice cracking under the weight of what he is suggesting. While he may be right about the purity of emotion I have inside of me, I am not sure I am the right person to stand with him. There has to be more qualified and deserving angels for a position of this nature.

"I assure you, there is no one better than you for what I am suggesting. The position will change nothing. I will still need you to remain here in Heaven for the duration, but as eager as you are to change things, as well as learn and my eagerness at surrounding myself with your purity of heart, I do believe this will benefit not only Heaven, but every being above and below."

"I do not know what to say…"

"I am aware this is a lot of information to process. I am also aware that you do not believe yourself to be deserving of such a position but as I have already stated, you have more than proven yourself. Do this, Faith, not only for me, but for yourself."

"Who will look after the humans?" I ask, the only real question left to ask. I have heard what he wants me to do and I am more than accepting of it, but despite that, I will not walk away unless I am positive that the humans I have been charged with will be taken care of."

"They will be handled, and with the utmost care, I assure you."

"Then you already know my answer."

As he reaches out, placing his hand upon my shoulder I experience the feel of what is taking place before I see the full impact of it. His light surrounds us both now, and I feel his power fusing itself to mine. Hearing about moments like this does not do it justice. What is taking place now, both inside of me and around me, is truly breathtaking and I know that when it is over, I will be forever changed.

"Faith, daughter of heaven, bringer of light, I am hereby stripping you of the light needed in your assigned task of protector of humans, so that we may move forward, stronger and more determined in our battle with the darkness."

Chapter Seventeen

Michael

"Who will look after the humans?"
"They will be handled with the utmost care, I assure you."
"Then you already know my answer."
"Faith, daughter of heaven, bringer of light, I am hereby stripping you of the light needed in your assigned task of protector of humans, so that we may move forward, stronger and more determined in our battle with the darkness."

After leaving my brother, finally at peace now that I had accepted the truth as it had been laid out before me, I knew there was only one place I needed to be. Armed with the knowledge I had about what we were going through, I needed to see Faith, explain everything to her and then do all I could in order to repair everything that I had broken in my attempt to push down reality.

Appearing now, I see her standing with Father, the both of them conversing. Not wanting to interrupt what is taking place between them, I listen to the words being spoken and wait with baited breath for them to finish so that I can finally speak. It is only when I hear his final words and see the light being pulled from her that my blood runs cold.

Wasting no time, I move forward. I need to stop this before he drains her of the light completely. I need to make him see that what he is doing, is not the right end. I am the one that put all of this into motion. It should be me experiencing his upset now, not her. All she did was accompany me because it was her charge I wanted to go to the planet to save. She is an innocent and I refuse to let him treat her any other way.

"Father, stop! Do not take her light away! It is not her fault."

They both freeze in their positions at the sound of my voice and Father turns to me first, Faith following close behind, her eyes a mask of confusion and if I am reading emotions correctly, hurt. Hurt which I had been the one to cause her. All of this happening now, Father being here and stripping her of her position, it is all my fault and I need to make it right, even if I am too late.

"Michael—" she says before I quickly cut her off.

"Faith, right now there is nothing of real consequence that you could say that will change the situation so please refrain from talking."

I am aware of how it appears, my head overflowing with an influx of different emotions all rushing to the surface, demanding to be heard, making me appear far worse than I wish to be, but the truth in my words I will not apologize for. She needs to remain silent now. This is between me and my father.

"Excuse me? Who do you think you are? Telling me when I can and cannot speak. You have no idea what you have just walked into the middle of, Michael, so I do believe you need to be the one that is silent."

During our short time together, I have enjoyed our verbal sparring with one another. At times it had been combative, but usually it was just the two of us unable to see eye to eye. The way she is now, her eyes cold, no real emotion present in them, she is reminding me not of the angel that she was during our time together, but myself.

It is in this moment as I am here ready to defend her, lay all of what I feel at both her feet and Father's that everything Gabriel said comes full circle. She is most definitely my beloved. She is mine, which only makes what I need to do now that much more important.

"You may be willing to accept him stripping you of the light for what we did, but I am not. You do not deserve this end, not when everything that happened was put in motion by me."

"Michael, I do believe you need to listen to Faith. It appears as though you are misreading the situation."

"Did you or did you not just strip her of the light? Taking with it every bit of power she did have to save the humans you claim to care so deeply about?"

"I did."

"Then Father, I do not believe I am misreading anything. You need to undo what you have done here. This is not Faith's fault. It is mine. Strip me of the power, remove me from Heaven if you have to, but please do not take her power away."

The sheer torture I feel at just the mere thought of her being without the light that makes her the pure beauty she is, threatens to bring me to my knees, the intensity of it that strong inside me. I have not come to terms with everything just to have it ripped away from me before I can truly experience it.

This will happen over my dead body. If Faith is to be removed from Heaven for the rules we have broken then she will not go alone.

"What has been done, will not be undone, Michael."

"I cannot believe I am hearing you say this!" I spit at him before turning to face the other person in the room. "And you! You are not even fighting his decision. You know how all of this happened, why it happened and you do nothing to fight for your position here! You do not deserve this!"

Turning my back on both of them, unable to come to terms with everything that flows through me. I am angry with them both and though the reasons are different, I am aching because I am being given something yet having it taken away at the same time. For the first time since my creation, I feel powerless. I am completely and utterly powerless to stop any of this.

Her acceptance of her fate is burning a hole in my chest, one where I am sure my heart resides and I am dangerously close to crossing a line in an effort to make it stop. I cannot let this be the end, not before it has even begun. Father will not take her from me, he will have to kill me first.

"Michael stop this right now!" Fathers voice booms, breaking through my thoughts. It is only when I feel the binds, the full force of his power wrapping itself around me that I know what has to happen next.

If she is accepting this and Father will not go back and undo what has happened, then I can no longer be here. For centuries, I have been shown and taught that everything we do here is for the greater good, but right now, in this instance, this is serving the darkness.

Focusing my mind on what I need to do now, the flame appears in my hand and even though I know it will be no match for his own, I nurse the flame until it becomes a fully grown fire ball. With a silent prayer that it works as I need it to, I push it toward the binds and watch as the flames eat away at the energy Father has created. After a few moments, I am free of the binds. Turning and facing them one final time, I say the only thing left in me to say before disappearing right before their eyes.

"If you will not see the error of your ways, I am done. With everything."

Chapter Eighteen

Faith

"You may be willing to accept him stripping you of the light for what we did, but I am not. You do not deserve this end, not when everything that happened was put in motion by me."

Those words have been haunting me since the moment they fell from his lips and he disappeared before my eyes. Even with Father searching in every imaginable way for him, it appears as though he does not wish to be found. It has been days since everything came to a head and Michael is lost to us.

True to his word, I have been at Father's side as they attempt to locate him, but with each passing day, no sign of him anywhere, I am beginning to lose hope that he will ever be found. Father is aware of it, as when I seem to reach the lowest pit of despair at having a very large part of me missing, he seems to grip onto me tighter, giving me the strength I need to continue on when all I want to do is give up.

I am not the only one going through the motions, a part of me missing. Gabriel is reacting in much the same way and as hard as it is to deny, Michael is getting his wish because as we all search for him, both above and below, using the power to attempt to break through whatever walls he has placed around himself to keep hidden, I have grown closer to his younger brother.

What is taking place between us is not the way Michael imagined it of course, but I have no doubt that just like Michael and I are bonded together, the same can be said for me and Gabriel as well. It is after one of our talks that I put everything together that I know of the elder archangel and I start to realize that I have known where he is all along.

*****

"Gabriel, how much do you know about the beloved bond?"

"I have not experienced it myself, so I cannot tell you any firsthand information, but I do remember a great deal of what Father told us. What would you like to know?"

"How does the connection between the two of us work?"

"From what Father told us, it happens differently for all that experience it, so I am not sure I can answer that."

"Alright, well if we are beloved the way Father says and we have this connection that transcends everything both above and below, do you think if I reached out to him, I might be able to locate him?"

He seems to think about what I am asking, which only proves to me that he does not want to answer unless he has complete faith that his answer is the correct one. It means that whatever happens from this moment forward, I know I can trust him above any other.

"I do believe that if you tried reaching out to him and he responded to you, we might be able to track him. I would have thought Father would have tried that already."

"He did. Nothing came of it, but with nothing but time to think about this, I am starting to wonder if Michael remained silent on purpose. The last time he was here, he confronted us about me losing my light. He is upset with him so it makes sense that he would not respond."

"And you want to try again?"

"Yes, but this time I do not want to involve Father."

"That is not a wise move, Faith. I cannot stop you from doing it, but I feel that I need to warn you about what keeping this from him will cause."

"Nothing that happens to me can be as bad as what is happening now. Michael being gone, it is affecting me in ways I am not accustomed to. I do not feel like myself. I feel as though a part of me is dead and if I can rectify that, going against Father to do so, I need to do it."

"Well, if you are that determined to do it and my warnings will not deter you, than I suppose you know what you must do, but Faith..."

"What?"

"You will not do it alone. I will be with you every step of the way. Let's bring Michael home."

*****

Reaching out to Michael had not been easy. I was of the belief that just in closing my eyes and thinking of him, I would have been able to reach him, but Gabriel quickly dispelled that notion. Not only did I have to think about him, but I had to put all of my focus into the way that I felt when we were together. The desire he sparked, the brutal agony I experienced when he had told me that we were wrong for one another. I had to bring all of that to the surface in order to connect and even though I followed through, it threatened to destroy what was left of me in the process.

His response had not happened right away, which with the time that passed, left me feeling even emptier than before, but when I finally did break through to him, the connection between the two of us could no longer be denied. All of the negative emotions I had been putting myself through vanished at the mere sound of his voice, almost as if they had never existed at all.

*****

"It appears as though you have learned a great deal about our bond in my absence."

"You have not left me a choice. Michael, you need to come home."

"Has he restored your light?"

"No, but there is much you do not know about that..."

"I witnessed all that I needed to. Until such time as he returns the light to you, I will remain locked away, where none of you will get to me. What he has done, it is wrong Faith and I cannot allow him to have his way, even though it breaks my heart to do so."

"Your heart does not need to break, do you not see? I am telling you that what you witnessed is not what you believe it to be. Come home to me, please."

There is a moment of silence following my plea and I fear that the connection between us has been broken. It is only when I hear him sigh that my mind is able to calm and I hold out hope that he will do as I have asked.

"I cannot do that. Do not reach out to me like this again, Faith. It is better right now that we are apart."

*****

I did not agree with what he asked of me and there was no way I would bend to his request now that I had been made aware of all that exists between us, but I was not about to tell him that. The communication between us ended on that note, but what he does not realize is that I was able to pick up on his location and now not only would I not listen to his warning, I am going to handle him face to face.

Handling all of this without Father finding out had been difficult, but true to his word, Gabriel had come through for me. In a matter of minutes after I explained all that I knew to him, he had my vessel arranged and he was prepared to bring me to the planet.

That is what Michael had been trying to hide and been unable to. He had not hidden out anywhere in Heaven, or some random location on Earth. No, he had gone back to the one place that would mean something to not only him, but me as well. So, not only do I know that he is safe, I also know that he is doing right by the human boy we helped only a few short days before.

Michael is with Colin, and soon, he would not be alone.

Michael

When I disappeared from before Faith and my father, I had no clear destination in mind. At first I just transported myself to another part of Heaven, one that was not inhabited by any beings and one that had no plans to be. It was from there that I decided on my next move and even though I knew at any point that I could be found out, there was no other place I needed to be.

Everything that has taken place in the short time since I had been home, had been caused because of the beloved bond between Faith and myself. It is only natural that I go back to the place where it all began. There might have been signs of it in Heaven before we had even come to stand before Colin, but it was here that I touched her for the first time, brought my lips to hers and ignited what had been boiling under the surface.

I know a great deal about the bond we share and I am also aware that because of that connection, she will be able to locate me, breaking through the walls I have put up to keep myself hidden from my brothers and father. I should be concerned about Father using that to his advantage and reaching out to me, but I am not. I do believe I know Faith better than that now. I may not know all there is to know about the ball of light, but in this way, I instinctively know she will not betray me. For doing so would not only hurt me, but bring the pain I experience down on her as well.

"You're back? I swear to you, I haven't touched a thing since the two of you left. I've been doing my best to stay clean and get my shit together."

"I am not here for you, Colin. I needed to remove myself from a volatile situation and this is the place I feel most comfortable."

"Squatting in an abandoned building is where you feel most comfortable?"

"As preposterous as it sounds and believe me it is, yes, this is the place I feel most comfortable at present."

"Does it have something to do with the other angel that was with you?"

"I am unaware of what you mean."

"Why you feel comfortable here? Is it because of Faith?"

"No, of course not." I answer a little too quickly. I have never been much for lying and it is apparent in how quickly I try to make light of his words that it has no plans on changing any time soon.

"Not very convincing."

"I care little about what you are convinced of."

"So, it is about her. You came back here because of her. Look, I'm a guy, I get that you don't wanna talk about this kinda shit, but man, it's written all over your face. She cares about me, so even though you don't want to, you care about me too."

"Has anyone ever told you that when you are cleaned up, you are too perceptive for your own good?"

"If by perceptive you mean smart, than yeah."

"Please refrain from trying to figure me out."

"Not much to figure out, you're laid out pretty open right now man."

"Yes, I am here because of Faith. Does that make you happy? Can we please stop this topic of conversation now?"

"Does she know you're here?"

After reaching out to me the way she did only minutes ago, I have no doubt that she is aware of my location now. I am just not sure what she plans on doing with it. I may believe that she will not take this to Father, but I could not hide the reality that I do not know her as well as I claim. There is no telling what she will do with the information or if she will even be able to return here at all.

"She is aware of it, of that I have no doubt. Whether or not she shows up, that I cannot answer."

"She's in love with you…" he says, more in statement than question, as if it is just common knowledge that even the dullest form of human life can figure out. If Colin is aware of this information, it means he has known even longer than I have and that is just unacceptable to me. I cannot accept how blind I have been.

"She may have been at one time, but after the way I have behaved with her, both in our time here and back home, I am not sure she feels the same any longer."

"I can't believe I'm the one saying this, but I don't think you could do anything to her that would stop her from caring about you. I mean look at how far gone I was and she never gave up on me and it had nothing to do with love or a connection."

The boy does seem to understand quite more than I have previously given him credit for. His words speak truth. She does care a great deal about the boy and there is no bond between them other than him being her charge, a being that she must take care of during his time here. It is the opposite with me. I only hope that when we do come face to face again, things can be made right the way he says.

With everything I have been feeling since coming to the realization with Gabriel, I cannot accept it being any other way.

As I prepare to respond to his statement, informing him that I could not agree more with what he believes, I hear the creak of the door beneath us, growing louder as whoever enters pushes it open as far as possible. My body tensing, preparing for whatever awaits us, more than ready to protect the boy and make sure that no harm comes to him, I move forward.

While I am positive that no one but Faith knows of my location, that does not mean that Lucifer has not been tipped off in some way to my arrival on the planet and is sending his own method of attack my way. I want nothing more than to decompress from the events of the day, no battles looming over the horizon, but it appears that I am not going to be afforded that small request.

It is only when the person reaches the top of the stairs and I am able to see them that I realize it is not one of Lucifer's henchmen after all, but the very angel that I have been unable to get out of my mind since the moment she walked into it weeks before.

Faith is here and if the look on her face is any indication, she is not at all happy to see me.

Chapter Nineteen

Faith

When we first touched down, I assumed Gabriel would be accompanying me for the duration. Considering all that I had learned about my lack of power when taking a vessel, not to mention allowing Father to take the light from me days ago when he removed me from my bringer of light position, I figured that I would not be allowed to be on my own.

As it turned out, Gabriel did not wish to stay, trusting me to handle this myself, but not before saying his piece, words he had spoken to me on one previous occasion, but that had more meaning now that I have been made aware of everything.

"I do not want to leave you alone, but if I remain here with you, Father will learn of the deception and right now, I believe that is the last thing either of you needs."

"What will you tell him when you have returned?"

"That you are doing what is needed to bring Michael back to us."

"Do you really think I can do that? Bring him back?"

"You are the only one that can bring my brother home again, Faith. Now that he has been made aware of what is happening between the two of you, his home is wherever you are. So do what I know only you can, and bring my brother back to me, the way he is meant to be."

Standing here now, face to face for the first time in days with the archangel that owns not only my heart but the very soul that lives inside of it, I am afraid I am going to somehow falter and what Gabriel wanted of me, I will not be able to do.

Knowing that of all the places in the world he could have hidden himself away, he chose to do so here, it means everything to me. Colin is so much more than a human that I needed to watch over. In caring for him, fighting to bring him back and seemingly failing at every turn, he had almost become an obsession for me. Saving him at one point had become my entire reason for being and Michael choosing him to reside with, well it spoke volumes to what the archangel must be facing.

I want to believe that he chose Colin because of the connection to me, but I can never be that selfish in my thinking. The only way for me to know the truth though is to open my mouth now and speak the words I have been going over in my head since I located him. The words that just do not seem to want to come. So instead of doing what I know needs to be done, I do the next best thing.

I turn my attention to Colin.

Just in the time since we have been away, he seems to have changed a great deal. The marks that coated his body, some of them open wounds at the time, are now closed over and on the mend. Where his skin had been devoid of color before, it is now a bright shade of pink, a warm smile coating his features in the very light that we had brought him back into. He looks alive, for the first time since I have been placed with him and I could not be happier about it.

The satisfaction that comes with knowing that I had a hand in this, it flows so strongly inside of me that I am afraid that at any moment I will burst from the sheer force of it. I had done this, at least in part. I had saved this beautiful human being and given him another chance at a life he did not feel he deserved to live. As long as I exist from this moment forward, I will carry Colin with me always.

"If it isn't the most beautiful angel in Heaven. I was wondering if you were gonna show up."

It is not standard protocol, what I do next, but the way he smiles at me, and the warmth in my heart at seeing him lit up so brightly before me, there is no way I can stop it. Turning from my place at the top of the staircase, I run toward him, not stopping until I am in his arms and embracing him as tightly as I can manage. It is only when he lets out a chuckle and I can see his cheeks darken that I realize my reaction has embarrassed him. Not wanting to cause him any further discomfort, I pull away, but not before returning his smile with one of my own.

"You are looking well, Colin. I am sorry I did not come sooner, but I am breaking rules even doing it now."

"And you aren't even here for me."

This human, he is a perceptive one, of that I am sure. Though I am sure, given the way I reacted at coming face to face with Michael again, it is probably more than a little obvious my real reason for being here. It is not as if I could hide it, even though I had attempted it for a few minutes.

"No, I am not."

"I'm gonna get out of here and give you two some space, but Faith, go easy on the guy. I get the feeling that whatever it is he did, it happened because he doesn't have the first clue about how to deal with people. Even other angels. I figure if you treat him like an infant, it makes a whole lot more sense and you can get through to him better."

I cannot help but grin at the way he calls Michael a baby, though I do no relish turning around and seeing the archangel's reaction. I cannot imagine it makes him happy at all hearing what a being that he considers less than him thinks.

"I do not believe him to be less than me, Faith."

"Like I said, I'm gonna get out of here. It's obvious the two of you need to work some stuff out."

Before I have a chance to thank him for giving us this time, or even to say goodbye, he has made himself scarce, the only sound that he is even still in the confines of the building, the sounds of his shoes as they hit the stairs on the way down, each step taking him further away. A few short weeks ago this might have caused me discomfort, but now, I just know that wherever he finds himself, he will be okay.

"The human is right. There are some things we need to discuss."

My body freezes in place as he speaks, prepared to hear it yet still unsure what it is that I am going to say in response. It had been so easy before I touched down, working all of the words out in my head, but now, standing here, it is as if everything I had worked so hard on has vanished and I am left completely devoid of any real thought process at all.

"Maybe you can start by telling me why you came here?"

"I could not remain at home, you must understand that, so where else was I to go?"

"I am aware that you felt you needed to leave home. I meant, why did you come to Colin? Surely there are a million other places you could have found yourself that are catered to your way of being."

"I came here because it is where I am most comfortable."

"If I ask you to explain that, will you do it?"

"For you, I will do anything."

His words, they reach right into the parts of me that have most felt the loss of him and they do as I am sure he intended, healing me, warming me. They break down the very large walls I have spent centuries creating until I am completely at his mercy.

"I came here because despite my desire to escape all things related to home and to you, it appears as though that is not what my heart wants. I needed to be here so that this moment, what is taking place this very second, could occur."

"You came here so I could find you?"

"Precisely. I may have wanted to get lost, to Father, to my brothers and the other beings of Heaven, but Faith, I never want to be lost to you."

Michael has always had a way of being honest. He may do it in a way that is very curt and sometimes borders sarcastic, but he is nothing if not honest at all times. He is speaking his truth to me, but even knowing that, I am shocked to my very core at how open he is. He is for the first time since we met, allowing himself to feel and it takes everything within me not to run to him the way I did Colin only minutes before.

It may be the connection, a beloved bond causing the reaction in me, but no matter the reason, it no longer matters. All that does is that I have never wanted to embrace a being more than I do Michael.

"How did you manage to get out of Heaven and into this vessel again without alerting Father?" he asks, bringing me back from the aching need I am experiencing and putting my focus back on the here and now.

"Gabriel. He was with me when I called to you and he would not let me do this alone."

"When you return home, you will pay for going against him. Why take the risk?"

"I think you know the answer to that, Michael."

"You sound a lot like Father."

"What is that supposed to mean?"

"He never tells us anything when he believes we know the answer already. I asked you a question and you, like him have assumed I already know the answer. Would I have asked if I knew of it?"

"Yes, because I do not think it is something you want to admit knowing."

"Please, enlighten me to what it is you believe I do not wish to acknowledge."

"Our bond."

"I assure you," he says with a dry laugh. "I have acknowledged and accepted the bond between us. My question to you, about taking the risk, is about more than the bond at this point is it not?"

"Michael, I cannot read your mind, so just spit out what it is you want me to say."

He is talking in circles and I am becoming annoyed with it. It appears as though I am not dealing with one archangel but two different ones and the up and down of it all is nauseating.

"That is where you are wrong, ball of light. You can reach into my mind in a way that no other being in existence can. It is how you were able to figure me out so easily the last time we found ourselves in this exact location. So, if you wish to know what it is that I want you to say, read me and find out."

I do not need to read his mind to know what he wants me to say. It is exactly what I want to say to him, but the fear I have at not having it returned, despite his earlier comments prevents me from doing so. What he wants me to admit, I have never experienced before and despite how secure I am in what I feel, I cannot help feeling scared about what it means moving forward.

Bridging the gap between us, until his body comes to rest directly in front of mine, he reaches out to me and raises my chin until his eyes are all I can see. It is looking at him this way that I see everything crystal clear. All that he has kept hidden from me since the very moment we met is there, shining with the light surrounding him and there can be no more running or hiding from it.

"You see it do you not?"

"I do."

"Then tell me, why did you risk further punishment coming here this way?"

"Because no matter how far you go, how separated we are, I am unable to escape the fact that I am in love with you."

"There it is…" he says, the words coming out significantly different than his normal baritone that I have become so familiar with.

"There is what?"

"The truth."

"Michael, this is all so new to me. I have only learned about everything a few short days ago. Is it too much to ask that you stop talking in riddles and really speak to me in a way that I can understand?"

"I have wandered the planet for days. I started out doing it at home, until it became too much and I made my way down here. I watched over Colin for a while, but when that became too much for me, I would roam various other parts of the planet, in an effort to escape you and all of these blasted feelings you have brought alive in me. No matter how far I went though, I always ended up right back here with the boy, because despite my every attempt at running from this, from you, I cannot seem to do it. Faith, the truth is, I am in love with you and even though I am concerned about what it means for us in the future, I am done running."

Michael

Now that I have opened myself up to her this way, there can be no stopping me. I can see that what I have just admitted to has stunned her into silence, but just as quickly as she seems to react to the words, she blinks those exquisite brown eyes at me and I know she is about to respond. It is something I cannot allow her to do just yet.

There is still so much that needs to be said.

"What happened when Gabriel found us locked in the embrace, deep inside I knew what was happening between us, but I had not yet reached a point where I could admit to it openly. So I did the only thing I could and turned on you. It is not the first time I have turned things around in that manner with you but it is one instance I am ashamed of. I am sorry for treating you that way. Before you vanished, I felt your heart break, something I did not even realize was possible and it was in that moment that I knew."

"You knew what?" she whispers, her eyes again locked on mine, no longer blinking, completely focused on my every word.

"What we were to each other. That I loved you. Gabriel may have felt that he had to talk me into it, but that was only because I could not bear to speak the words aloud at that precise moment. Faith, I believe I have known what has been happening between us long before we even left Heaven, but I was too stubborn to admit it. Even now, I am finding it hard to find words to adequately explain to you what it is I am going through."

"Try Michael. I need to know."

"The thought of you with Gabriel, even when I was the one suggesting it, the rush of blood to the head I feel when I am in battle, it happened then, but it was worse. I physically wanted to take my brother and rip him limb from limb every single time I pictured the two of you together. The heat that both my human vessel and my true form experiences whenever I am within a couple of feet of you, it is enough to drive a crazy person sane. I have never wanted to be around another being so much in my entire existence. Even now, standing here with you this way, not touching you is enough to make me want to explode."

I am fully prepared to continue, but before I can even open my mouth to take the breath needed in order to get the rest of what needs to be said out, she pulls away from where my hand rests on her chin and she rushes into my arms, until all I am able to feel is the sensation of being totally complete.

"What is it that you feel right now, as you stand here, holding me this way?"

"I feel whole. You make me whole, Faith."

"If that is the truth and I have never known you to be any other way, you know what has to happen next."

"I cannot do that." I answer immediately, knowing what she is getting at and not willing to agree. I know it is only natural with me admitting how I feel that it is time I return home, but like I told her before, that will not happen until things with her have been put back the way they are meant to be.

"Yes, Michael, you can."

"No, not until Father fixes that which he has broken in taking your light away."

"It is time you learn the truth about what you walked in on."

"I do not need the truth, I already know what that is. Faith, if I never return home again and Father does as I know he will do, stripping me of the power and light, I need to know something."

"What is it you need to know?"

"Will you live a life with me here, as one of the fallen, even though I know it is not what you are meant for? I know it is a lot to ask and you deserve so much more than a lifetime lived in that way, but I cannot imagine my life without you in it."

"It will never come to that, but yes, Michael. If we had to live this way in order to be together, I would do it in a heartbeat."

Before I can ask her what she means, saying that it will never come to that end, I sense it and my blood instantly runs cold. The concern I had before her arrival that Lucifer would send someone due to my entrance to Earth, is rising to the surface again. We are not alone. He has indeed sent someone.

"Get down!" I yell, knowing she will not understand what is happening but needing more than anything to keep her safe.

She hits the ground just as the orb of fire crashes through the side of the building and throwing my body down on top of hers, I pray that I am able to get her out of here before harm comes to her. I have no idea who it is that I will be dealing with when he makes his appearance, but I do know the last thing that I want to happen is for this beautiful woman, angel, my ball of light to be caught in the crossfire.

"I need to get you out of here."

"I am not going anywhere, Michael. Whatever this is we will face it together."

"Faith, now is not the time to be stubborn," I snap, pushing down the reaction my body is having to the way she moves under me. "I have no idea what we are about to face and you are without both light and power. I need to get you out of here and I need to do it now."

"Without power or not, Michael, I am not leaving you to fight alone."

Faith

I don't know how long we lay crouched on the floor of the warehouse, but I do know that Michael being over me the way he is, protecting me in the only way he can, is causing things to happen inside of me and none of them are things I am familiar with.

Where a situation such as this would have frightened me before, it is not now. I want nothing more than to push the archangel off of me and face down whoever is waiting for us. I could rise and find that it is Lucifer himself that is here and it would not matter. If there is a choice between fight or flight, I am going to fight and there is nothing Michael can say or do to change it.

His body is stiff and rigid as it covers mine, and it is filled with nothing but heat, causing my very human vessel to sweat and not in a tolerable way. It is another reason that I need him to take himself away from this position now because the longer I am forced to sit here in my own sweat, and heat, I do believe I will combust.

"Well this is not what I expected to walk in on, but I cannot say I am all that surprised."

The voice that is speaking, I am not familiar with but it appears as though with the way Michael tenses that he knows the voice well. I want to reach out to him now, using our bond in the most basic of purposes and ask him who this person is to him, but before I can even attempt to focus my mind, Michael is rising up and turning his back to me.

"Faith," he whispers as quietly as possible. "Call to Gabriel. I am aware that it may not work but please, you have got to try. I need to get you out of here."

"I told you, I am not leaving you." I answer, no longer concerned with whether or not I am being stubborn, only knowing that I am not leaving him alone to fight this. He has been dealing with things for far too long alone, now that he has me that changes. He may believe me to be weak, but now, in this moment I have never felt so strong.

"Samael…"

Samael is a name I know. It is the very angel that Michael had been sent to destroy before helping me with Colin. How he is standing before us now, I have no idea, but it does not look as though I am going to have to wait long to find out. The angel is nothing if not forthcoming.

"It appears as though the fire you called on to end me, did not work in your favor. All it did was give me what I needed in order to truly join with the side of right."

"Choosing Lucifer will never be right!" Michael exclaims before turning his body back toward me, his eyes giving away the concern he feels in the moment, having me here with him and being unable to protect me the way he wants.

"Call Gabriel, Faith."

"If I was not witnessing it with my own eyes, I would not believe it. Michael, protecting a human. Will wonders never cease."

Samael begins taking steps toward us and Michael, doing all that he can in order to keep me safe, pushes me backwards and as I stumble to keep myself upright, I see a sword appear in his hands and my stomach sinks. I have always known what Michael is, what he is guided by, but to see it firsthand, I am not sure how I feel about it. He will always be a warrior but that is a part of him that I do not want to witness. I do not enjoy hearing, let alone seeing the bloodshed that he must deal with on a daily basis.

"You will not get another step closer to her, Samael. I may have failed in removing you the last time we met, but I will not fail again."

"Oh, brother, how adorable you sound defending the honor of the very being that will be your downfall."

"You know nothing!"

"That is where you are wrong. I know everything and mark my words. The very human that stands behind you now, will bring you to your knees. She will destroy all that is right about you until there is nothing but the darkness left."

Again the dark angel moves, but this time there is a weapon in his hand, shining under the light of the sun now blasting its way through the gaping hole in the building, landing directly where Michael stands.

Somehow sensing what is about to come next, Michael moves forward and in one fluid movement, lifts his sword until it meets with Samael's and they begin the fight. They go back and forth, meeting each other at every turn until Samael spins around and gets the upper hand, knocking the sword from Michael's hands until it clatters to the ground in front of him.

My breath catches in my throat as I watch him dive for it, but as he does, I see Samael coming up on his left and not thinking, I scream Michael's name so loudly, he has no other choice but focus on it and not on the weapon he is so desperate to get to. It is only when he comes to stand again, blocking Samael's sword with his bare arms, that I see the blood begin to spill and some instinct inside of me rises to the surface so strongly I am powerless against it.

Pushing forward, I throw my body into the fallen angels until he is stumbling to keep himself grounded. I claw at him, using my very human fists to hit him until he finally falls backward. It is only when his body hits the ground that I turn to face Michael and see that what I have done has indeed given him the advantage again.

Not only is the sword back in his hands, but the wounds that Samael had just inflicted have already begun to heal. Running to him, he grabs a hold of me, pulling me tightly into his arms before lifting me up completely into his arms.

"I have no idea what has possessed you to act in this way, Faith, but whatever it is, thank you."

"I told you, I will not let you go through this alone. Now do what you did not get to do the last time. Finish him once and for all. End the darkness."

Placing me down on the ground, with one squeeze to my now shaking hands to let me know he intends to do exactly as I have said, he turns back to where his fallen brother had been laid out only seconds before. It is only when he comes face to face with the empty floor that we both realize that in our haste to connect, we lost sight of what was important. Samael's words had been correct all along. I was going to be the very thing that would bring Michael to his knees. In allowing this bond to ignite the way we did, I have surely put him on the path to his true death.

Seeing the shadow out of the corner of my eye, catching it before even Michael can become aware of it, I am standing face to face with the angel that only minutes before I had taken to the ground. Moving forward under a force that is not my own, unsure of exactly what I am going to do with no weapon or power at my disposal, the angel smiles at me, copying my own movements and making his way toward me.

"Faith, move!" Michael screams at me, but even though I hear his words and want nothing more than to break away from the path I have found myself on, I am locked completely in place. The fear begins rising to the surface and I realize what is happening.

Samael has somehow gotten control of my body and he is using it in the manner that is bound to hurt Michael most. He is going to drag me toward him in an almost slow motion state and he is going to end my life.

It is in that moment of realization that I know what I must do. I only hope that it works as I intend. Michael may not like it, or even agree with what I am about to do for him but there can be no going back. Using all of the strength I have inside, I push myself toward the shiny blade resting a few short feet from me and as it plunges straight into my heart, taking not only Michael but the fallen angel off guard, I know that I have succeeded in what I set out to do.

I have done whatever was needed to give Michael what he would need to finish off Samael once and for all, even if I had gone to my own true death to do it.

Epilogue

Michael

Somewhere out there, living freely among the humans, going about their business without a care in the world because they are cloaked and hidden from me is a demon. One of the highest order in Lucifer's army and the very demon that put the scene that is now taking place before me in motion.

I know nothing of where he is, but I am aware of who he is. Samael, the man I once called brother, the very angel I stood beside on many an occasion as we fought the darkness. He is responsible for what is happening now and when I am able, he will pay.

If I had known that things would turn out the way that they have, I would have freely given myself over to him because there is no being alive less deserving of this fate than Faith.

Despite my need to be on my own, both Father and Gabriel have attempted to speak to me since I walked through the gates, her still and cold form pressed as closely as possible into mine. They want me to see their truth, the one that no matter where I go from here, or what I do, I will never see.

This is what I know. In agreeing to help Gabriel the day he came to me, insisting that I speak with the bringer of light before taking steps to rectify the problem with the human boy, I put her on this course. If I had just stayed away from her, the beloved bond never would have ignited and Faith would still be enjoying a long luxurious existence in Heaven where she belongs. She would be helping the humans the way that only she can and not lying here now, as cold as ice, locked inside of her human vessel, completely lost to me.

We never would have had a reason to interact, therefore the bond between us, the very thing keeping me here right now would never exist. That is my truth, it is what I know as fact, even though to hear Gabriel and Father tell it, it is nowhere near the truth.

They want me to believe that the bond would have ignited regardless of how and when we interacted and that this moment we find ourselves in now, was destined to happen from the start. It is that very thing, the idea that this was written into her existence that I refuse to believe. How can someone as pure of heart as her be destined to experience something as violent as what she has? There is nothing right about that.

Even with the passage of time, I can still see her walking toward me, accepting me as I am, even though I am nowhere near the being that she deserves and the primal scream that escapes her throat as she realizes what is about to happen and jumps in the way to stop it. I can see the blood as it begins to stain the front of her outfit, starting slow and then pooling in a large round circle the more that escapes. Catching her before she has the chance to hit the ground and cradling her tight and close in my arms, feeling her final breaths as they escape through her slightly parted lips.

It is then that I wrap her form up as tightly as possible into my own and I go home, even though with the way I left things, it is the last place I want to be. As efficient as I am as a fighter, a warrior for my Father and all of Heaven, I am not the healer of the family. That honor is bestowed upon not only Gabriel, but Raphael and it is to them that I bring her, silently praying that I have not wasted too much time and they can bring her back to me. To all of us.

I am unsure of what I will do if they come to tell me that there is nothing more that can be done. I do not think, given all that I know now, I can survive it. If Faith passes before I have the chance to tell her what she means to me, what she has brought to life inside of me just by being the ball of light that she is, it will be as though a large piece of me has died to. That is how connected to her I am. One cannot exist without the other.

Pulling myself away from the thoughts that haunt me, yet ones I do not need to be focusing on with Faith fighting for her life mere steps from me, I see Gabriel making his way toward me, his face displaying nothing that can prepare me for what is about to happen. I want him to appear broken, or smile so I will be able to tell which way this is going to go, but he does not oblige me.

"Michael…"

"If you are here to tell me that she is lost to me, do not say another word."

"She is not lost."

"Say it again brother."

"Michael, I was unaware that hearing was an issue for you." He smiles at me as he says the words, not as brightly as I have seen him do in the past, but it is all I need to see moving forward. It is that smile he is displaying as he attempts to put me at ease with a joke that allows my heart to steady and I begin to believe in something again.

Where I had been feeling lost mere moments before, now I am filled with something I never thought I would ever feel again.

I am filled with hope.

"Faith is going to be okay. We were unable to save the vessel, but we were able to separate her and use our combined power to heal the damage that has been done. It was touch and go for a while, but it appears as though the healing took and she is on the mend."

"I care very little for the vessel."

"I expected that answer to be honest, just do not let Father hear you say that. The vessel was pure, just as Faith herself is and it is a loss that even though I did not know her, I feel just as I am sure Faith will when she awakens again."

"Gabriel, I need to see her."

"I figured that. Raphael is finishing up with her, but when he has completed what he needs to do, I will not keep you from her."

"Thank you."

Gabriel embraces me, fusing his strength and power with mine, giving me back what I had not even realized I had been missing. He is giving me my light back. Faith being injured, now that the bond had been ignited between us, had caused my light to dim, an experience I should have known to expect, but paid no mind to. It is just another thing I had to thank my brother for.

"Michael, there is something that you need to know."

"Unless it pertains to that angel in there fighting for her life right now, I do not wish to hear it. Anything else can wait."

"It is about her."

I can feel the ache beginning to build inside me again, preparing myself for whatever Gabriel is about to tell me. He may have said she was okay but that did not mean that there was not something else going on that could prevent her from making her way back to me.

"As we were healing her, we were able to tap into her mind, her thoughts and feelings. Michael, what her and Father were talking about before you arrived, she was not being punished. She was being promoted."

Promoted? Remembering what I walked in on, there is no way what I witnessed could have been anything but Father stripping her completely of the light she was born with. What he is saying does not make sense.

"I know what I heard, Gabriel. He stripped her of the light."

"Yes, he did, but not of all of her light, just the light needed in order to help the humans. You forget that she did not start out there. She was originally created as a ball of energy. It is only when Father chose a different path for her that she ended up where she was."

"So he was not punishing her?"

Gabriel shakes his head and my heart sinks. Not only had I misread things between Faith and my brother, but I had also done the same with my father and in the end been the very reason all of this is happening now. Had I just stayed and listened, none of this would have happened.

"Do not do that to yourself Michael. This was always meant to happen. Maybe not in this exact way, but it had to happen in order for you to get where you are now. Just as you could not have prevented what happened with Samael, there was nothing you could have done to stop Faith's choice to give her life up to save yours."

As I am about to respond, a shadow overtakes our light and turning in the direction that it is coming from, I come face to face with the other brother that had done all that he could to save my beloved's life.

"You can see her now, Michael."

Faith

Two things become apparent the minute I am finally able to open my eyes again. The first comes as no surprise because from what I can remember of my final moments before everything went dark, he was there with me, but the other thing takes me completely off guard.

Where we had been in an abandoned building the last time I was coherent, now we are not. With the light shining from Michael as he stands over me, whispering words he is unaware I am able to hear, I can tell that we are no longer on Earth, but instead back home in Heaven.

It had not happened the way I wanted it to, but seeing him now, even though my eyelids are still heavy, weighted from the ordeal I have been through, fills my heart with happiness. He is back at home, the place where he should always be, just the way Gabriel wanted him to be, at least in part. If he has been returned to the way that he used to be, I have no idea, in fact there is not much I know at all after the sword sliced through my chest, but I can only hope that I have delivered him in the way Gabriel wanted.

Seeing him now, taking in his rigid stance over me, his body language speaking to the tension and concern he feels, I want to reach out to him. Let him know in some way that I am awake and aware of him being here and it is him being here now that is making me feel stronger by the second. I want to question what happened to Samael after I blacked out, wondering if he had been taken care of the way I hoped for in doing what I did. I want to tell him how much I love him, but opening my mouth to do so, nothing but the smallest breath of air comes out.

That is all it takes. He lifts his gaze up to my face at the escaping sound and where his eyes had been focused yet distant mere seconds before, now they are filled with light, and if I am not mistaken, there is the barest of smiles lifting his features. His eyes flicker over mine, searching them for a reason I cannot understand.

"Please tell me that I am not dreaming this." He whispers, leaning his body down over my own and placing a tender yet soft kiss to my forehead.

It is far from a life altering move for most people, but knowing Michael as I do, the small motion he makes in giving me a kiss melts my heart. As resistant as he had been before to what was taking place between us, it appears that everything we have been through has softened him now to a point where he is beginning to accept it.

I want to tell him that he is not dreaming this. I am indeed here, awake and looking back at him with the same amount of devotion and adoration as he is displaying for me, but the words will not come.

"Raphael warned me that it might take a little bit of time before you were able to speak. The ordeal you have been through has taken a lot out of you. I am just so happy that you are awake. You frightened me for some time with as long as you have been out."

Focusing my mind and all of the strength that I am slowly starting to gain back, I force my hand to move until I can see it lifting out towards him, not stopping until I feel it connect to his face. If I am unable to speak, I will handle it, but there is no way seeing him as I am now that I will handle not touching him in some way. Seeing the way his body relaxes under the soft brush of my hands across him, warms me in a way I never thought I would get to experience again. The magnitude of it growing as he leans his face into my palm, answering my need for feeling with one of his own.

"I thought I lost you…"

Pointing with my other hand toward him, than shaking my head and pointing back at myself, I pray he will understand what I mean until I can find the strength needed to be able to speak the words aloud to him. When his eyes shine and he smiles, I am again hit with a wave of warmth, a happiness that we seem to be able to speak to one another without any words being necessary. This is the beloved bond in its finest form and it is one that I never want to lose.

"It appeared as though for a while, losing you was a very real possibility. Faith, I have no idea what you were thinking doing what you did, but as long as I live from this moment on, I never want to experience something like it again. I am amazed I am even standing here now with what happened the minute the sword pierced your skin."

I shoot him a look of confusion, one I hope that he is able to pick up on so that he can explain to me what he means by his final words, and he does not disappoint.

"Our connection, the way that it works is that if one of us is seriously wounded, whether in battle or in some other manner, the other will experience it twice as badly. There was a few minutes after you fell to the ground where I was sure Samael would win and I would never get to experience the way it feels right now, seeing you this way."

"I—sorry." I manage to choke out after using every bit of energy I had in order to make even the barest sound appear.

"You have nothing to be sorry for, dove."

"Samael?" I ask, wanting to know more than anything if the fallen angel had been taken care of the way I hoped.

"He escaped, but only because I was more focused on getting you home than taking care of him again. Nothing else mattered."

For the first time since waking up, I am unhappy. The whole point of me taking control back from Samael had been to rectify the situation Michael found himself in. I wanted him to finish the angel off once and for all so that the evil that truly resided within him could be wiped away forever. Knowing now that Michael had foregone his end in order to see to me, is enough to make me want to fall back into the deep sleep I have just woken from.

"There will be another time for Samael and me, dove. Please do not ever think of going into the abyss that way again. I will not allow it. I will never allow it."

"Ending—him—more—important."

"Even now, with you at your weakest point, you attempt to be stubborn. I am aware that we are beloved, dove, but now is not the time to act like me. Now is the time to be yourself again. The warm, caring and loving being I am so consumed by. The one I cannot imagine living this existence without."

"I—need—to-tell—truth."

"About what?" he asks, his expression never changing even though I am positive that he does not know everything there is to know about what happens now.

"Father."

"I am aware of everything as it pertains to the conversation between you and Father if this is what you are alluding too. Gabriel informed me of everything."

"You know?"

"I know it all angel. It appears as though for a short time, I am going to have a partner by Father's side and I could not be happier about it."

"You mean that?"

"I have never meant anything more. Before our conversation got interrupted, there was still so much that I wanted to say to you. Maybe now is the time for me to do that."

I nod, wanting to say more but my voice not cooperating enough in the moment for me to get it all out effectively. I am willing to hear all that he has to say as long as keeps him the way he is now. I know that in time, he will go back to the way he has always been, but this part of him, the way he is with me, I want it to remain forever, even if the rest of him changes.

"If you are not meant to be a bringer of light, then there is no other place in all of Heaven that I want you then by my side. It is where I need you to be because when I am with you, even though I am experiencing things I am most unfamiliar with, I am strongest. I spent so very long running from that fact but I can do it no longer. What Gabriel told me that day before I found you with Father is true. You do not weaken me, you just enhance what is already there. It is by my side that I want you so that I can truly be the warrior I have always been meant to be."

"I love you, Michael."

"Of that I am aware, light of my heart. It can only be compared to that of the love I feel for you, though I am sure what I am experiencing is cataclysmic compared to your own."

In his own unique way, he is telling me that he loves me more and it fills my heart with joy. What is taking place between us is something that in my wildest dreams, I never would have expected to experience. We have both been forever changed by it, in the purest way possible and I want nothing more than to heal quickly so that I begin to live whatever comes next.

"Gabriel has explained to me that I am not to push you, so I do believe I will leave you now, let you rest so that when I do come back, we are able to spend more time together, but Faith, there is one thing I need to know before I take my leave. I want you to answer me in your mind so that you do not force too much too soon."

What do you want to know? I ask, doing as he has requested and taken to answering him in a way that is easier for the both of us.

"Why did you throw yourself onto the blade? I can think of numerous reasons why you would have done it but for the first time since I have met you, I do not want to misread, or assume anything."

Samael was able to control my movements, he was forcing me to take the steps toward him. I saw what my end would be if I continued to allow it so I did the only thing I could in the moment. I threw myself onto the blade so I could protect you. I needed to keep you safe.

"You are the most stubborn angel I have ever come across."

That might be the funniest thing you have ever said to me.

"Faith, you could have been lost to me forever. Promise me that no matter where we go from here, you will never put yourself in the line of fire again. I cannot bear the thought of losing you. This was too close of a call and it is one I will not repeat."

I promise.

"You are my beloved and as such, I will go to the ends of the earth, or even my true death in order to keep you safe. I know you want to do the same, but just this once, concede to me and let me be the one to protect you. Let me do that which I have been made to do."

I already said I promise, Michael. Do not push me any further than that.

Before he can react to the annoyance I display, I smile at him, letting know in a way that does not need to be spoken that I mean nothing by what I am saying. As annoyed as I expect he will make me during our lifetime together, it is something I embrace and not something I want to ever turn away from.

"I will take my leave now. You need to rest, so that I can take you from here as soon as you are better and begin our life together."

"Don't leave…"

Whether it is the pleading sound of my voice, or the frantic look in my eye, I cannot be sure, but his eyes soften and leaning into me, as close as two people can possibly be, he presses his lips to mine tenderly, never once closing his eyes, instead keeping them trained on me, watching as I react to his touch. After a few seconds locked in the same position, he pulls away, but not so far that I feel the loss of him.

"I will never leave you again."

The End…

Follow Michael's story as it continues… Fall 2014

Hold Onto Me Playlist

M.I.N.E (End This Way) by Five Finger Death Punch

Miracle by Shinedown

Stormy by Hedley

Be Here by Parachute

City of Angels by 30 Seconds To Mars

Heaven's Gonna Wait by Hedley

23 by Jimmy Eat World

I Won't Let You Go (Darling) by Hedley

Warning Sign by Coldplay

Hear You Me by Jimmy Eat World

Weight Of The World by Framing Hanley

Always by Saliva

Stay by Rihanna (featuring Mikky Ekko)

Castaway by Framing Hanley

I'll Follow You by Shinedown

Hold Onto Me by Mayday Parade

Acknowledgements

Jennifer Kendrick. This book would not have been written without you. Your love of Michael can only be compared to mine and it is because of you asking the questions, wanting to know more that this story came to life and will continue long after the final page has been read. Here's to you and to Michael living on forever!

To my wonderful children, I love you. You continue to put up with Mom's weird hours and moods while she's writing and for that, you've proven what I've known all along. You really are angels brought to life.

Faith Walsh. This story was originally dedicated to you because when I picture Faith, her strength, her emotion, her way of being overall, you are the vision that comes to mind instantly. I changed it at the last second but I do believe that being acknowledged for the amazing friend, person and mother you are is infinitely better than my original dedication would have been. Here's to you and all that you are. You are loved, remember that always.

Joey, thank you. For never letting me give up, keeping me moving forward, reminding me of the reasons why I started this crazy endeavor to begin with. There is so much more you need to be thanked for, but those are tops. I love you and I will treasure you always.

Mallory Osmun, never give up on your dream. Keep writing stories that you want the world to read and no matter how scary it seems, never be afraid to share them with the world. I have no doubt that you'll change the world with your words the same way you have already done in the short time I've known you.

Theresa Troutman. I am thankful to know you, to have access to your expertise and to support you as your take your own journey into the crazy world known as being an author/writer. You're truly an inspiration and I hope to travel this road with you for more years to come.

Lisa Wilson. You may live on the other side of the world from me, but there is no doubt that we're sisters and no matter how much time passes, how many books I write, we'll always remain sisters. Thank you for your constant support of me and for allowing me to be a part of your reading experience every step of the way. You're amazing. Never forget that.

To every person that spends their money and time on this book or any of the others I've written. From the bottom of my heart, I first want to say thank you and then tell you that I love you. Yes, each and every one of you. Thank you for taking a chance on me and sharing it with me. You're the best readers a girl could ever have and I will be forever humbled by all of you.

About The Author

Melyssa Winchester is a mother of four from Toronto, Ontario, Canada. When she's not knee deep in adolescent awesomeness, she's falling in love, one book boyfriend and girlfriend at a time. She is a lover of all things romance and will forever believe in a real and true happily ever after.

When she's not off being a mom or writing you can find her doing one of two things. Reading or buried under the covers watching Supernatural, Sons of Anarchy or Veronica Mars.

Melyssa is currently working on Before The Light Book #2: Absence Of Light (Ryan's story) that follows the lives of the characters from the Love United Series before they came together. She is also hard at work on a standalone title Shades of Blue and working on All My Heart (Kayden and Isabelle's continuing story from Count On Me.

You can find her on the web, either at her personal site, Facebook (which she just might have an obsession with) or Twitter (@WinchesterBooks) where she talks incessantly about her kids, her writing and all things book boyfriend related.

Other Works by Melyssa Winchester

Love United Series

1. Holding On To Heaven

2. No Surrender

3. Wanted

4. Stairway To Heaven

5. A Light In The Dark

Before The Light Series

1. Hold Onto Me (Michael's Story)
2. Absence Of Light (Ryan's Story)
(coming June 2014)
3. Iridescent Vengeance (Lucifer's Story)

Count On Me
(Available Now)

My Heaven
(Holding On To Heaven Alternate Ending)
(coming soon)

Hear Me Now

(Coming June 2014)

Take Me With You

Shades Of Blue
(Coming July 2014)

All My Heart
(Kayden & Isabelle's Story)